MASTER
OF MORGANA

Allan Campbell McLean

COLLINS · LIONS

First published 1960 by William Collins Sons & Co Ltd
14 St James's Place, London SW1
First published in Lions 1974

Printed in Great Britain
by William Collins Sons & Co Ltd, Glasgow

MASTER OF MORGANA

'I stopped, panting, straining my ears for all they were worth. Above the loud thumping of my heart, I was certain I could hear the sound of hurrying feet scuffing the loose gravel on the road. I took to my heels. I was half-way down the road before I caught sight of him . . . Right away I knew he was my man.'

At that moment, sixteen year old Niall knew that his brother's near fatal fall was not a mere accident. Someone had fully intended Ruairidh to die when he fell deep into the gorge. But why should anyone want to rob quiet and solitary Ruairidh of his life? Move by move Niall is bound tighter in a web of intrigue and suspicion.

Set against the lonely, rugged background of the Isle of Skye, this is an immensely gripping adventure story for older readers, especially boys.

'Mr McLean writes like John Buchan at his best. You just cannot put it down. It gets an alpha plus.'

Times Literary Supplement

OTHER TITLES IN LIONS

A LIKELY LAD *Gillian Avery*

THE GREATEST GRESHAM *Gillian Avery*

THE WARDEN'S NIECE *Gillian Avery*

THE HILL OF THE RED FOX *Allan Campbell McLean*

THE YEAR OF THE STRANGER *Allan Campbell McLean*

THE MOCK REVOLT *Vera and Bill Cleaver*

ELIDOR *Alan Garner*

THE MOON OF GOMRATH *Alan Garner*

THE WEIRDSTONE OF BRISINGAMEN *Alan Garner*

THE OWL SERVICE *Alan Garner*

THE OUTSIDERS *S. E. Hinton*

THE HAUNTED MOUNTAIN *Mollie Hunter*

CLIMB A LONELY HILL *Lilith Norman*

THE GUNSHOT GRAND PRIX *Douglas Rutherford*

NO WAY OF TELLING *Emma Smith*

and many more

To
Dr. Anne Gillies

Chapter One

It was the longest day of the year, but we never saw a blink of the sun. A strong wind out of the north brought sudden showers of cold rain, and there was a heavy sea running. Hearing the rumble of the surf on the shore, I thought of my brother Ruairidh and the rest of the crew at the salmon fishing station. With the sea so wild they would never manage out with the coble to fish the nets, and I wondered if Ruairidh would get home for the day, if there was no fishing.

It was Midsummer's Day, and I remember it well, but not because of the weather. That was the day they carried Ruairidh home on a rough stretcher, pale as death, his black, curly hair matted with blood from a great open gash on the back of his head.

I had just finished feeding the calves, and was making back to the house with the empty pails slung over my arm, when I heard a shrill whistle. I glanced around and saw Iain the Post standing by the fence at the top of the croft, beckoning urgently to me. I put down the pails, and started the long trail up the croft to him, wondering idly what he wanted, for he had been to the house with mail earlier in the morning.

It is queer how you can sniff trouble on a man. Iain the Post never said a word at first, just took off his peaked cap and passed a hand across his bald head, jammed the cap on again, cleared his throat, and spat on the grass, all common enough actions that I had seen him do a hundred times before. But this time I knew that something was wrong.

'What is it, Iain?' I asked.

'There has been . . . an . . . accident, boy,' he said slowly, picking around the words as if he had a hard job putting his tongue to them. 'It is Ruairidh. He is hurt.'

'Ruairidh? Hurt?' I repeated stupidly. And then: 'Is he hurt bad?'

'Bad enough,' said Iain the Post, his round, red face grave and set.

I felt a quick stab of fear. 'What happened?'

'It seems that Ruairidh fell off the bridge across the gorge,' he said, avoiding my gaze, and peering down at his boots as if he had never clapped eyes on them before. 'He struck the rocks, poor fellow, and he was near drowned before they got him hauled out of the river. I doubt . . .'

I waited for him to go on, but he remained silent, moodily digging the heel of his tackety boot into the soft turf. 'Well?' I said.

He gave me a long, searching look, and said shortly: 'They are bringing him home. I met them back the way.' He jerked his head in the direction of the track that wound over the hill to the main road. 'You had best warn your mother, boy, before they put in an appearance.'

'I believe it would be better for you to tell her, Iain,' I said miserably, 'seeing you know all about it.'

He studied his boots again, and swallowed. 'I had best phone for the doctor,' he said at length. 'The nurse is out. Away and tell your mother. I will be over as soon as I get word to the doctor.'

I turned to go, but before I had covered ten paces he called: 'Niall!' I swung round. 'Ruairidh is unconscious, mind,' he said quickly. 'And he has a terrible grey look on him. You will need to speak to your mother, boy, or the fright she is in for is something awful.'

I nodded, and made off down the croft to the house, stricken dumb more by the look on the face of Iain the Post than the words he had spoken.

Our house stood at the foot of the croft with its back to the rising moorland and the cliffs and the sea. I looked at it as if seeing it for the first time, thinking how it must have looked to Ruairidh, homely and welcoming when he came back after a long spell at sea in strange parts.

It was a good solid house of grey stone, with a slated

8

roof and three storm windows on the upper story. My father had built it himself with stone quarried from the hillside, just as my great grandfather had built, long ago, the little thatched house behind the stackyard that was now our byre.

I wondered if Ruairidh would ever again race me down the croft to the house, and the thought made me sick in the stomach. I stumbled on, unseeing, tripped over the taut tethering chain of one of the calves, and sprawled headlong in the grass.

The calf scampered away, the swivel creaking as he strained on the tether. I scrambled to my feet, furious with myself, and ran the rest of the way to the house.

My mother was kneading dough on the kitchen table, shaping it into a big circular scone. Her bare forearms were dusted with flour, and her face was flushed a bright pink. She brushed a wisp of hair out of her eyes with the back of her hand, leaving a smudge of flour across her forehead, and glanced up at me. 'Good life, boy, the memory you have!' she scolded. 'Amn't I for ever telling you not to be leaving the feeding pails out on the croft?'

I sat down on the old wooden bench facing the gleaming black range. The peats were red and glowing, and a scone was baking sweetly on the girdle. 'I forgot,' I said.

My mother's hands were busy with the dough. 'A pity I am not forgetting your dinner,' she said. 'There would be some racket then, I am telling you.'

'Ruairidh has been hurt,' I said.

Her strong, square hands dug into the dough, and she bent forward over the table, her grey eyes searching my face, repeating the words I had used myself only a few minutes earlier, but saying them in a whisper. 'Ruairidh? Hurt?'

'He fell off the bridge over the gorge,' I said quickly. 'They are bringing him home now. Iain the Post told me. Iain is away to phone the doctor.'

My mother's eyes closed and her whole body seemed to droop, as if a weight had been put upon her that she could not support. It was barely two years since my

9

father had died, and I suppose she felt it hard having to face this trouble without him by her.

She straightened slowly, easing her hands from the dough and stripping it from her fingers. 'Is he hurt bad?' she said dully, wiping her hands on her apron.

'Bad enough, if he fell from the bridge into the river,' I said, 'what with the terrible drop and the rocks lying below.' My mother's eyes closed again. 'But Ruairidh is as strong as a bull just,' I added quickly. 'He will be up and about in no time at all, you see if I am not right. It would take more than a fall off a bridge to put Ruairidh on his back for long.'

'Aye, he is a strong boy, Ruairidh,' she said, but there was no conviction in her voice, and her face looked stricken.

I got up and put an arm about her shoulders and gave her a squeeze. 'Good life, you know fine he is the strongest man in the place,' I declared confidently. 'Cheer up, now. If he sees you looking like this, it will be enough to make him weep.'

But when they carried him into the kitchen it was myself who could have wept.

He was lying on a stretcher that had been hastily fashioned from some pieces of rough timber and a length of old sailcloth. He was wrapped in a couple of faded grey blankets, and his face was near enough the same colour, except that it had a waxy look. Someone had folded a jacket and placed it under his head as a pillow. The jacket was stained with blood, and his black, curly hair was matted where it had seeped out of the deep gash in his head.

His breathing was so shallow that I had to put my face close to his before I convinced myself that he was not dead. I brushed a lock of wet hair back from his forehead, feeling his skin cold and clammy to the touch.

'Out of the way, Niall,' my mother said calmly. 'Put him down in front of the fire, boys.'

Willie MacLeod was at the head of the stretcher, and a tall, red-haired fellow supported the other end. Big

Willie lived in our township; he and Ruairidh had worked together at the salmon fishing station. The red-haired fellow was a member of the crew, too. I had heard Ruairidh say that he came from Harris, but this was the first time I had seen him.

They lowered Ruairidh gently on to the rug in front of the fire and stepped back, rubbing their cramped hands and looking down at him. My mother went down on her knees beside the stretcher and started to fuss with the blankets.

'Mind his leg now,' Willie said awkwardly. 'The right one. It has taken an awful crack, and the shin bone is through the skin. The skipper put a sort of a splint on it, but it is a job for the doctor.'

My mother nodded, stroking Ruairidh's forehead with gentle fingers. It was the way she used to put me to sleep when I was small and had wakened, crying and fretful, in the night.

'But how did it happen?' I demanded, unable to believe that Ruairidh of the cat-like tread, so light and agile on his feet, could ever have slipped and fallen.

Big Willie rubbed at the black stubble on his chin with a hand the size of a ham. 'I can't make it out,' he said slowly. 'The bridge is bad, right enough, but Ruairidh was a smart man on his feet. I never saw the like of him. I suppose he got careless just.'

'Were you with him when he fell?' I asked.

'No, I was in the bothy. We couldn't get out to fish the nets. The north wind had raised a swell that was something awful. Ruairidh said he would meet Lipton's van on the main road, and get cigarettes, and off he went. I was lying on my bunk when I heard Long John let out a roar that would have raised the dead.'

'Long John?'

'John MacGregor, the skipper,' Willie explained. 'Seeing he has only one leg and a crutch, he never gets anything but Long John, like the fellow in the story – Long John Silver. But not to his face, mind. Well, when I heard that roar I near fell out of my bunk. I hauled on my boots and made for the door. Long John was tearing for the river – the same fellow is handy with the crutch; he can move faster than many a man with two good legs. He plunged right in and struck out for the rocks near the bridge. The next thing I saw, he had Ruairidh by the neck of his jersey. Oh, but for Long John the big fellow was drowned, that is a sure thing. Murdo here and I dragged the pair o' them out.'

'Aye, that was the way of it,' the red fellow said. 'It was some job, too, carting him up from the bothy.'

Well, the climb out of the gorge with the stretcher was a deal easier than having to dive into the river to rescue a drowning man, I thought, particularly with Big Willie leading the way, Willie who had shoulders on him like an Aberdeen Angus bull.

I studied Murdo, the Harris man. He had a long, foxy-looking face, and the pale, cold eyes and thin lips that often go with red hair. To tell the truth, I did not fancy the look of him. It was no wonder to me that a man with one leg had got to the river before him.

The door opened quietly and Iain the Post came in with my sister, Morag, on tiptoe behind him, and three other men from neighbouring crofts. Morag started to cry when she saw Ruairidh. I was wild with her, weeping in front of all the men, but my mother soon quietened her.

'The doctor is on his way,' Iain said, 'and the ambulance has left Portree, so it won't be long until Ruairidh is safe and sound in Broadford Hospital.'

'The sooner the better, or I doubt he is finished,' Big Willie said softly to the red fellow; but not softly enough, for I could see by my mother's face that she had heard.

One by one the men of the township gathered at our house as the word of Ruairidh's accident got around, until there was a crowd in the kitchen and more besides standing out in the lobby. But the doctor soon shifted them.

He came striding in, his kilt swinging, and hustled the whole crowd of them outside. He tugged at Morag's plaits. 'You too, lassie,' he said, smiling, 'and be quick about it.'

I had never seen a broken leg fixed up before, and I

was trying to peer over the doctor's shoulder without looking too nosy, when my mother took me aside. 'Away and change into your good clothes, Niall,' she whispered urgently. 'You will need to go with Ruairidh in the ambulance.'

I went upstairs reluctantly and changed into my good suit and the white shirt with the stiff collar that I had got for my cousin Duncan's wedding.

When I came down again my mother met me at the door and took me across the lobby into the other room.

'Is Ruairidh . . .?' I started fearfully.

'The doctor is seeing to him,' she said quietly. 'Here.' She pushed two notes into my hand. 'You will need money to get yourself a bite of food, and for the bus back.'

'Ach, I am not needing food,' I protested.

'Wait you until it gets round to evening, and I doubt you will be after changing your mind,' she said, smiling a little. 'I want you to stay at the hospital until it is time for the late bus to Portree. Maybe Ruairidh will be – well, maybe he will be better by then.'

'What does the doctor say?'

'The doctor thinks he might have a fractured skull,' she said. Her voice was low, but it was steady enough. She might have been telling me that Ruairidh was needing to get a tooth pulled. I marvelled at the calm of her, she who was liable to lose the head supposing I was an hour or so late for dinner, or some little thing like that, of no account at all.

'Is he still unconscious?' I asked.

She sighed. 'Aye, and he might well be for days, so the doctor says. But they will tell you better when they have seen him at the hospital.'

I was gazing out of the window, watching the men waiting outside the house. Seeing them standing there in small groups, talking softly, not laughing or joking, put me in mind of a funeral. I did not like it.

My mother said: 'Who is that coming down the croft?'

Through a gap in the rowan trees that circled the house, I saw a man striding down the croft. He had a rolled stretcher over his shoulder and a nurse was hurrying along by his side. We went back to the kitchen. Ruairidh was moved carefully to the proper stretcher, and there was no lack of willing hands to grasp the handles.

My mother walked with us to the main road where the ambulance was parked, and the last words she said to me were: 'Be sure to go to the hotel now, and get yourself a meal. Donald Stewart says he will meet the late bus in Portree, and drive you home. And Niall – ' she squeezed my hand, and for the first time I saw tears in her eyes ' – mind and bring back Ruairidh's clothes with you. They are in a terrible state just, soaking and torn and blood all over them. I wouldn't like them left in the hospital.'

Any other time I would have liked fine the long drive to Broadford, through Portree and Glen Varragill, right under the towering mass of the Cuillins at Sligachan, and all the way round lonely Loch Ainort. But I had no eyes for the country, and less thought. Indeed, all I remember of that journey is seeing a heron standing in the shallows of Loch Ainort, still as a rock, and thinking to myself how sad he looked; that, and the moment when the driver swung off the main road into a narrow, tree-lined side turning, and said: 'Well, son, this is Broadford Hospital.'

I should have been relieved once we reached the hospital, but I felt more miserable than ever, seeing Ruairidh whisked inside, surrounded by uniformed nurses, and not having anyone to talk to now that the driver had disappeared, too.

I hung around outside, staying close to his ambulance, not wanting to lose contact with the only man I knew in the place, walking up and down on the pebbled path, trying to look as if I had a purpose in being there. I had almost given up hope of seeing him again when he suddenly appeared on the front step. He seemed surprised to see me. 'You still here, son?' he said. 'Better go down to the village, or you might miss the afternoon bus. It won't be long now.'

'I think I will wait for a while yet,' I said.

'Well, you might as well take the weight off your feet,

eh?' he suggested, taking me by the arm and leading me round the side of the hospital. He pushed open a door and pointed to another. 'In there.'

I opened the door and found myself in a bare room with chairs around the walls. An opening at the far end led into a long corridor. I sat down and waited.

From time to time, nurses hurried past, but none of them took any notice of me. A man in white, wearing a long rubber apron and rubber gloves, hurried through the little room where I sat, two nurses hard on his heels. A woman who looked like a cleaner poked her head around the door, smiled at me, and went away again.

I don't know how long I sat there, or how many nurses hurried past. I lost count of the number of times they went by. Every time I plucked up enough courage to speak to a nurse they were past me before I could open my mouth, although I suppose that is just my excuse, and I was really afraid of tackling them.

I lost all count of time. I felt as if I had always sat in this room, as if I were doomed to sit there through all the years to come, unseen by those passing by, like stories I had read of people in olden times the fairies had put a spell on.

When a nurse finally stopped, and said, not unkindly: 'What are you waiting for, laddie?' I could only gape at her stupidly, lost for words. She said again: 'What are you waiting for?' but speaking this time in Gaelic instead of English.

I got to my feet clumsily, feeling my face reddening. 'I was waiting to hear word of my brother, Ruairidh,' I said. 'He was unconscious.'

'Oh, aye, the fisherman,' she said slowly. And then, sharply: 'Have you been waiting here ever since he was brought in?'

'Well, no, I was waiting outside for a whiley,' I said hesitantly. 'The ambulance driver told me I could wait here.'

'Do you know what time it was when your brother was admitted?'

I shook my head.

'Barely two o'clock.' She glanced at her watch. 'It is now eight-thirty. You must be starving.'

'No, I am not hungry,' I said, thinking of the untouched notes in my pocket, and afraid she would think I was without money. 'If I had been hungry I would have gone to the hotel.'

'Well, it is too late for the hotel now,' she declared. 'Come with me.' And before I could open my mouth she marched off briskly.

She took me into the kitchen, and a homely looking woman, who put me in mind of my mother, gave me a plate of soup and a feed of potatoes and cold meat, and after that a dish of ice cream. Ice cream in a hospital! For sure, Morag would never believe me when I told her.

When the nurse came back I thanked her and the other woman for the food, not knowing whether I should offer to pay, but afraid to do so in case I offended them. My mother would have taken it on the nose if a stranger had offered to pay for food she had provided, and, as the woman in the kitchen had a look of her, I thought it wiser to hold my tongue. But I did ask the nurse about Ruairidh.

She said he was still unconscious, and had a suspected fracture of the skull and a badly broken leg. If I phoned in the morning, they might be able to say more.

She came out to the door with me, and said suddenly: 'Your brother is very ill, you know. All we can do is hope – and pray.'

I nodded, and turned to go. It was then that I remembered Ruairidh's clothes. The nurse took me back inside and pointed to a lighted window along the familiar corridor I had gazed down for the best part of the day.

I tapped on the window, and when it slid back I told the young nurse who appeared what I wanted. She looked surprised, and asked had I not made a mistake with the name. I said no, surely, I would not make a mistake with the name of my own brother.

'Well, that's queer,' she said, frowning. 'A young fellow called for his clothes not five minutes ago. He said he was a friend. Perhaps he didn't know you were here. But if you hurry you should catch him all right.'

I mumbled my thanks and raced out of the hospital. At midsummer in our island it is usually light until almost midnight, but a wet mist had drifted in from the sea, and what with the mist and the overhanging trees on the road, I could not see very far ahead. I ran down the road as fast as I could go, and I must have covered a hundred yards before I realized that the thief might have taken another turning.

I stopped, panting, straining my ears for all they were worth. Above the loud thumping of my heart, I was certain I could hear the sound of hurrying feet scuffing the loose gravel on the road. I took to my heels again.

I was half-way down the road before I caught a sight of him. He must have heard me, because he had drawn into the shelter of a tree, and was looking back. Right away, I knew he was my man by the parcel that he clutched under his left arm.

He looked some size, but I told myself that was the effect of the mist; it could make a poor looking goat take on the shape of a bull. And, to tell the truth, I was that wild at the thought of him trying to lift poor Ruairidh's clothes, I would have made for him supposing he had been a giant.

As soon as he saw me, he darted between the trees, scrambled up the bank, and vaulted over the stone dyke. I took the bank in two flying strides, and leapt the dyke. Ruairidh is always having me on because I am a bit short in the leg, but even he has to admit that I can run. And I believe I never ran faster in all my life, not even the time I broke my stick on the bull and he turned and charged me.

The ground was rough, broken with old furrows and coarse tussocks of grass, and there was a fierce slope down it. Of the two of us, I believe I was the more used to hill country. At any rate, I was gaining on him fast. He glanced back and stumbled, and I was within ten yards of him before he had righted his stride.

'I'll get you,' I shouted in fury, and at that he flung

down the parcel.

I am sure about that. He did not drop it, not at all. He flung it away from him, knowing that I would go for it, and he would have a better chance to make good his escape.

But I was past the parcel before I could stop. I went down on my knees in a skidding turn, and scrambled back and pounced on it. By the time I had picked it up, the mist had swallowed him.

I stayed where I was for a time, getting my breath back and trying to take my bearings. The ground sloped steeply to the bay, so if the thief had kept on, his run must have ended in the sea. That puzzled me for a while. Why should he have run for the shore, which was a dead end, instead of trying to get away by the road, or over the fields in the opposite direction?

In the distance I heard a long, low whistle. It came from the direction of the bay, and it was repeated a second time. Then I heard the deep chug-chug of a diesel engine. There was a boat moving below me, close inshore, and on a night of thick mist when no seaman in his right mind would have moved a cable's length unless he had to.

I suppose I was tired and a bit shocked by all that had happened, otherwise I do not see how I could have been so thick in the head. At any rate, I know I had found my way to the main road and boarded the late night bus for Portree before I started to think straight. Indeed, the bus had rounded Loch Ainort before it dawned on me that Ruairidh's working clothes were not worth stealing. But there must have been some reason for a man to risk jail so that he could lay hands on that parcel of torn and blood-stained working clothes.

'Don't be a clown,' I told myself. 'It was not the clothes he was after. He must have been hoping to find something in them.'

I was sure I had hit upon the truth, and I was of half a mind to start raking through the parcel there and then, but there were too many people on the bus for that. I stuck my hands in my pockets, and thought a bit more.

I wondered how Ruairidh had fallen off the bridge in broad daylight. It had been raining, right enough, and that might have made the narrow plank bridge greasy underfoot, and treacherous to a man wearing heavy rubber boots. But Ruairidh knew the bridge like the back of his own hand, and he had a great head for heights. I would have backed him to cross the bridge blind-folded, for he had a tread on him that was as sure-footed as a cat.

I think the bus had reached Sligachan before I started to wonder if it might not have been an accident. But that meant that someone had tried to kill Ruairidh.

As soon as the thought came into my head, I tried to drive it out. 'What proof have you got?' I told myself, not wanting to let my imagination bolt on me like a runaway stirk. Indeed, I had no proof, none at all.

It was the diary that really started me thinking. But that came later.

Chapter Two

Donald Stewart was waiting for me when the bus came into the Square in Portree, his old Austin car parked boldly in front of the Police Station, which I thought was foolish, seeing that the licence had expired two years back, and there were things about the car the police would not be pleased with, supposing they were to inspect it closely.

Once we were out of Portree, I asked him why he had left the car in front of the Police Station. He laughed, and said something about people never seeing what was thrust under their nose, and I said I would not be so sure, not with the police, and he said he once knew a man who cut the label off a beer bottle and put it into the licence holder on his car and went around with it for years. I believe he was sorry it was not himself who had thought of that one. He had a good nerve, Donald.

We had passed the lochs and were climbing the hill that

wound around the cliff edge, when the exhaust hit the road with a clatter. Donald found a piece of wire and tied the loose exhaust to the bumper, but before we had covered another mile the lights failed. I thought we were stuck then, but Donald soon found the trouble. He had a lead held in position by a broken matchstick, and the match had worked loose. He broke a fresh match in two, secured the lead firmly, and we got going again.

We had talked about poor Ruairidh until there was no more to say about him, and I suppose I had started to brood. Donald broke the silence by saying: 'I doubt Big Willie won't stay long on the job now that Ruairidh is in hospital.'

'Why not?' I asked.

'Good life, who would stay on at the fishing with a great idle cratur of a Harris man to carry on your back, and the skipper a cripple just? If it had not been for Ruairidh, Big Willie would never have been there in the first place, anyway.'

'But surely they will get someone to go in Ruairidh's place,' I said.

'Never the day,' declared Donald. 'He was good for the work o' two men – aye, and three, if it came to the bit – but how many are there the like o' Ruairidh? The salmon fishing is a job where you need a good crew – four strong men, and able ones at that, or you might as well never go near the nets. Amn't I after telling you that the skipper is a poor cratur of a cripple, and the red fellow bone lazy? Surely you have heard Ruairidh speak of the Harris man?'

'No, he never said a word to me.'

'Well, I have heard Big Willie speaking of him; aye, and laying off his chest plenty about the same fellow not doing his share at all, at all. Loafing just, whenever he got the chance, and the cripple too soft to check him. Besides, how can they hope to get another man? No one in the place would ever stay in that bothy.'

'Ruairidh stayed in the bothy,' I said.

'Aye, so he did.'

'Well?'

'Ruairidh did many a thing the rest of us would never tackle. Never mind Ruairidh.'

'Well, he stayed in the bothy,' I persisted.

'Aye, but did Big Willie stay in the bothy? Not on your life! Big Willie came home every night.'

'He had cattle to see to,' I said.

Donald made a noise in his throat as if he would have liked to spit. I believe he would if only he could have got the window open. 'Cattle!' he exclaimed. 'Two cows and a stirk, and himself with three brothers at home! Are you wise, boy? Good grief, it was not the cattle that took Big Willie home from the bothy every night.'

'What, then?'

'You know well enough what it was that took him home,' said Donald darkly. 'Aye, and would take every other man in the place home, too.'

'Old wives' tales,' I scoffed. 'Fine I know them. Knockings and queer noises in the dead o' night down at the bothy. Timbers creaking when the air is still and the sea dead calm, and maybe a terrible cry now and then, like a drowning man might make before he went below for the last time. I am telling you, it is nothing but a lot of old wives' tales.'

Donald was in long trousers before I was born, and I thought he would be wild at me for being so scornful, but he only said soberly: 'I mind my father talking about it, and that was not yesterday. Everyone in the place knows the stories about the bothy, and the queer noises that are heard in the night.'

'Aye, everyone in the place knows about the stories,' I admitted.

'Well, why do you suppose they had to take on a MacGregor all the way from Glen Orchy, and another fellow from Harris,' Donald went on, 'when there are more than enough men here in the place eager for work? I will tell you for why – because there is not a man in the place would stay a single night in that bothy. Good life, I would like to see you there, boy, for all your big talk. You would never sleep a wink, I am telling you. Those noises would drive you out of your bunk quicker than if a fire was lit under you. You would be fleeing for home like a hare before the night was near done. Nobody could stand the like of those noises – timbers creaking on a still night . . . a drowning man's cries . . .'

'Ruairidh never heard any noises,' I said.

'How do you know?'

'Well, he never said a word to me about them.'

'The same fellow wouldn't be likely to,' Donald retorted quickly, 'seeing he was always making mock of the stories about the bothy.'

'Well, he slept there right enough,' I said stubbornly. 'You have got to admit that.'

Far out across the Minch a foghorn hooted mournfully.

'Aye, he slept there right enough,' said Donald grimly. 'And where is he now? Lying on his back in hospital, and near finished, unless I am far wrong, and I hope I am.' He shook his head and sighed. 'It is bad to mock at the stories of the old people, Niall.'

'Well, I don't believe them,' I said flatly.

He took his eyes off the road and looked at me, and shook his head again. 'You are a thrawn beggar, young Niall,' he said. 'I believe you would always go your own way, no matter what, once you set your mind to it. But mark my words, it won't be long before you see Big Willie leaving the salmon fishing. He may be a bit slow on the uptake, but he is not as thick in the head as all that.'

Donald parked the car in a passing place on the main road, and came over to the house with me. There was a crowd in the kitchen, waiting for news of Ruairidh; not that I had much to tell them.

I could see that my mother took the news hard. She had taken the parcel of Ruairidh's clothes from me, and she sat with it on her lap, her head bowed. I suppose she had been hoping that he would have regained consciousness, that I might have spoken to him, and brought her back a message from his own lips.

All the rest of them did their best for her, talking away as fast as any hungry pedlar, about men they had known who had lain unconscious for days and were none the worse for it afterwards. To hear them speak, and the long words they used, you would think there was not one among them that had not spent half his days working about doctors and hospitals and the like. But they were only trying to help, and it is a poor man who would not make a little lie to ease a mother's burden.

It was turned one in the morning, and the slow tick of the old clock on the wall above my head was lulling me to sleep. I was near dropping from tiredness, but I did not like to clear off to bed, seeing that Morag was still up, and looking fresh, too. But the neighbours did not stay for long once they had heard my news, and had satisfied themselves that they had cheered my mother a little.

When the last one had gone, my mother got up and took the big family Bible over to her chair by the fire. When our father was living we had readings from the Bible every week, but since his death we had got out of the custom. Not that my mother was not a religious woman; she was, but she did not read well, and I think she was shy of stumbling over the unfamiliar printed words.

She read to us from the sixth chapter of the Gospel according to St Matthew, and her soft, halting voice was still with me when I got into bed that night.

Take therefore no thought for the morrow; for the morrow shall take thought for the things of itself. Sufficient unto the day is the evil thereof.

I had heard those words before, many times, but I think I understood them then for the first time. I said the verse over to myself in the dark, and the words sounded well, spoken aloud, in a firm voice. I rolled over on to my side, well satisfied, and was asleep in an instant.

As soon as we had taken breakfast in the morning, Morag and I went down to the public call box on the main road to telephone the hospital. Morag did the talking, because she was better at the telephone than me. I always got a bit excited, and could never hear properly what was being said.

There was no fresh news, just 'no change.' Ruairidh was 'as well as can be expected.' If my mother was upset she did not show it. All she said was: 'Ach, well, we must just be patient, children. A bad knock on the head is not easy healed.'

But she went pink in the face when Donald Stewart came marching in, wearing his good Sabbath clothes, and said he had come to take her to the hospital in his car. She said no, she would never think of leaving Morag and me at home alone, and – when we protested – that she would be a bother to the nurses, fussing about the hospital.

For all her talk I could see she fairly fancied the idea, although it was a while before I realized that she was probably shy of going. Once upon a time, I did not believe she could be shy of anything. Then one day in Portree, I had seen her through the open door of a shop standing at the counter waiting to be served. She had looked small and frail and curiously uncertain, not a bit like the woman I knew so well who bustled around the house every day in life.

I had realized then that the house was more than a house to her. It was her kingdom and her fortress and once she was away from it she was not firm and resolute and sure of herself any longer.

Morag skipped around her, chatting: 'You are going to Broadford. You are going to Broadford,' and made to untie her apron. My mother pushed her away, half laughing, half scolding. But Morag kept on at her, and I joined in, too. Even Donald, who was an easy-natured man, not given to making up people's minds for them, did his best to persuade her.

In the end, she gave in. But the instructions she left us about the feeding of the calves and the hens and the pet lambs, and what we should eat ourselves! You would have thought she was away to Mars.

Once she was out of the door, and away up the croft with Donald, Morag said: 'Is Ruairidh going to die, Niall?'

I stretched out full length on the bench. When Ruairidh

lay on the bench his feet hung over the end, but mine were well away from it. Lassie, my black-and-white collie, tried to lick my face. I pushed her away.

'I am talking to you,' Morag said fiercely.

'I heard you,' I said.

'Well, is he?' she demanded.

'No.'

'How do you know?'

'I know well enough.'

'How?'

'Be quiet, girl, I am trying to think,' I said irritably.

'I suppose you have plenty more important things to think about than poor Ruairidh,' she said, angry tears starting up in her eyes.

'I was thinking about Ruairidh,' I said.

'Well?'

'Well what?'

'Well, how do you know he is not going to die?'

'Because he is not.' I slid along the bench until my feet were hanging over the end. 'Because he is Ruairidh. Because it would take more than a crack on the head to finish the likes o' him.'

She nodded doubtfully.

'Satisfied?'

She nodded again, and said: 'I suppose you are right, Niall.'

Good life, I never thought I would live to see the day when Morag would say I was right about something. It is queer how something terrible has to happen before people start to appreciate one another. Not that Ruairidh's accident had made me change my mind any about Morag; it was just that she had stopped giggling, and that was a relief any man would be grateful for.

'I am away out to see if the washing is dry,' she announced.

She came back loaded with a great armful of washing. She dumped it on the table, and I saw Ruairidh's torn blue denims and his fisherman's jersey. I sat up on the bench.

'What happened to the things out of Ruairidh's

pockets?' I said.

'The cigarettes and matches were soaked,' she said. 'We threw them away.'

'Was that all?'

She nodded. 'Except for a diary.'

'Show me.'

Morag crossed to the range and opened the oven door. 'I was drying it,' she said, taking out a small green diary and ruffling the pages. 'The back is a bit twisted, but it will soon be as good as new.' She popped it back inside the oven and shut the door.

'You had best see if there are any eggs,' I said.

'See yourself,' she retorted. 'I have got all this washing to iron and our dinner to get ready and plenty more besides. I would like to know what our mother would say if she could see you sprawled on the bench there, ordering me around.'

'Keep the head, girl,' I said. 'If you like, I will away and get the eggs for you.' I got up meekly and went to the barn where the hens had their nest boxes, and gathered the eggs.

My chance came when Morag spotted her friend Catriona coming down to the house. She was dying to tell Catriona that she had the running of the house until my mother got back, and she went racing out to meet her. I had the oven door open in a flash and the diary into my pocket the moment she was out of the door.

When the two of them came into the kitchen, I said I was going out to see if the cows had wandered. I cut through the fence at the back of the house, and made my way over the rough ground of the common grazing to the cliffs. I went past the break in the cliff face, where the old road wound down to the shore, and hurried on until I came to a small green knoll.

It was my favourite spot. Lying on the knoll, I could see over all the country for miles around; the long line of circling hills to the west, and the patchwork of crofts running down to the river. Every house in the district lay before me. At my back there were only the cliffs and the pounding sea.

I took out the diary. The soaking had warped the cover, and made the dye run, but the inside seemed to be dry enough. I flipped through the pages, and then went through it again, more slowly this time. I could hardly believe my eyes. The diary was blank. It did not contain a single entry.

I was of half a mind to stick the diary back in my pocket, and try to forget how I had allowed my imagination to lead me by the nose, but the stubborn streak within me insisted upon having a third shot. This time I licked my finger and turned over the pages one at a time.

I had reached the middle of May without finding anything when I discovered that several pages were stuck together. I prised them apart, and my perseverance was rewarded. There were entries for several weeks, starting at the end of May.

In the space for Sunday, May 30th, was printed the word 'MORGANA,' then there were numbers for every day in the week: Monday 11, Tuesday 47, Wednesday 35, Thursday 81, Friday 69, Saturday 105. It was the same on the next two weeks, starting on Sunday with the word 'MORGANA,' followed by a list of numbers. The last entry in the diary was on Sunday, June 20th – 'MORGANA.' There was no entry for yesterday, when Ruairidh had met with his accident. And the feeling was stronger than ever within me that it had been no accident.

I looked for some connection between the numbers, but there were only two the same; 81 against Thursday, June 3rd, and Tuesday, June 15th. I stared at the neatly printed numbers, trying to find some order in them, but there was none. It was all a meaningless jumble. And what did the word 'MORGANA' mean, repeated four times, on four successive Sundays? It sounded like a foreign place, but it was one I had certainly never heard of before.

All I could make sense of was the fact that the first entry in the diary was on Sunday, May 30th, and that was when Ruairidh had started to spend his weekends at the bothy. The salmon fishing season opened at the beginning of May, and, as the nets were not fished on the Sabbath, Ruairidh had started by coming home every Saturday afternoon, and not returning to the bothy until first thing Monday morning. But towards the end of May he had suddenly announced that he would not be coming home at weekends any more.

I had thought at the time that it was a strange idea, when there was no work to be done on the Sabbath, and from all I had heard the bothy was not a great place for comfort, just rough bunks, and bare stone walls, and draughts that would slice you in two when the wind was bad. But Ruairidh was not the man whose decisions you questioned, so I had kept my thoughts to myself, although I should have had enough sense to know that he must have had strong reasons for staying away from home.

I could see now that his decision to stay on at the bothy must be connected in some way with the entries in his diary, not the least with the word 'MORGANA,' which was repeated on four Sundays. If I could find where 'MORGANA' was, or what it meant, I would know why Ruairidh had thought it important not to leave the bothy.

I got to my feet, and made for home, my thoughts a queer mixture. I was puzzling over the diary and hoping that Catriona was still in the house. I liked Catriona. She was the exact opposite of Morag, tall and fair and quiet, not given to fits of silly giggling, or nonsense like that. But she was growing at an awful rate, which was a pity. I believe she had the beating of me by a good three inches, and that is terrible when you like a girl and she is only fifteen.

She was setting the table when I came in, and Morag said she had agreed to stay for dinner. I told her she must have a good nerve when she would chance Morag's cooking, but she only laughed. I expected Morag to get wild, but she was that proud at being left in charge, she just tossed her head and never said a word, for a wonder. When the two of them were safely in the scullery, I slipped the diary back in the oven.

We had fried chops and eggs and chips with fancy

rounds of sliced tomato. The chips and the sliced tomato were swank just; if Morag had been as busy as she made out, it would have been far easier for her to boil a pot of potatoes and serve the tomatoes whole. But I must say it was a good feed; I fairly enjoyed it.

'You are doing not bad at the cooking,' I said.

'It was delicious, Morag,' Catriona said warmly.

Morag got pink, and made a great show of gathering up the dishes. 'Ach, it wasn't much,' she said briskly. 'If only I'd had more time I could have made a proper meal with soup and a pudding and things.'

The girls washed the dishes and I lay back on the bench, trying, once more, to puzzle out the meaning of the entries in the diary. The thief who had tried to steal Ruairidh's clothes must have been after the diary, so the entries were bound to be of value. I was glad now that I had not said a word to anyone about my chase after him. Ruairidh had been working alone, that was a sure thing, and it was up to me to take over from him.

Catriona cut in on my thoughts. 'You are looking terrible solemn, Niall,' she said.

'I was thinking.'

'What about?'

'Oh, about Ruairidh. Who they would get in his place at the salmon fishing.'

Morag sniffed. 'They will have some job to lay hands on anyone,' she said. 'I believe they would be glad enough to take Kenneth the Soldier.'

Kenneth the Soldier was turned eighty, and near blind. I laughed, in spite of myself, and it was then that the idea first came to me, although I suppose it must have been hatching in the back of my mind ever since my talk with Donald Stewart on the way back from Portree.

'Well, I can tell you who will be going in his place,' I said, the words seeming to come out of their own accord, and not by any conscious thought.

They both looked at me. 'Not Donald Stewart?' Morag said quickly. 'He told me once that he would not stay a night in that bothy for a thousand pounds.'

I shook my head. 'It is myself,' I said.

They gazed at me with eyes like saucers.

'Away, Niall!' Catriona said doubtfully. 'You are having us on.'

'No, it is right enough,' I declared. 'I am going in place of Ruairidh.'

Morag started to laugh. Good grief, I never knew the equal of that girl for getting me wild. If Catriona had not been in, I would have set about her.

'You can laugh,' I said angrily. 'What way do you think we will manage here with no money coming in until the time o' the cattle sale, and that not until the back end, and Ruairidh maybe needing special things when he is home from hospital? Fine I could see you laughing all over your face if it was plain bread all the time on the table. Good grief, lassie, I believe it would take all my wages to keep you in food.'

That nettled her. She made a face at me, and said: 'You are after eating more for your breakfast than I take all day. Besides, you have never earned wages in your life.'

'Well, I am going to.'

She appealed to her friend. 'Did you ever hear the like, Catriona? As if they would pay that boy a *man's* wage.'

'Less of the boy,' I said grimly.

'Is it whiskers you are wearing then?' she retorted. 'Good life, what are you but a boy?'

'I am near seventeen.'

'You are not.'

'I am.'

'You are not. There is only a year between us. You are sixteen.'

'Near seventeen.'

I saw her counting on her fingers. She was thrawn that one. 'Sixteen and a quarter just,' she said.

'Well, sixteen – going on for seventeen.'

'Sixteen,' she said.

'Well, sixteen. What about it?'

'And you expect the Factor to take you on at the salmon fishing?'

'Why not?'

'And pay you a man's wage?'

'Why not?'

'The Factor would chase you.'

'No fear.'

'He would so.'

'He would not.'

'You would be sea-sick. Wouldn't he be sea-sick, Catriona?'

'Listen who is talking,' I scoffed. 'You would get sick, lassie, supposing I waved a piece of seaweed under your nose.'

'Ach, you are daft,' she said. 'Whoever heard of a boy doing a man's job, and a hard one at that?'

'I am as strong as any man,' I said.

'Poof!'

'I'll prove it.'

'How?'

'You'll see.'

There was an unopened sack of meal in the lobby. It weighed a hundredweight. I went out and dragged it away from the wall. The girls watched me from the kitchen doorway.

I bent down and got a grip on the bag near the bottom. It was not easy getting a good purchase, or even a right grip on the hard packed bag. I could carry a full hundredweight and more on my back, but I was a bit on the small side to manage a straight lift from the floor, and the thought of failure made me sweat. But I was determined to do it, supposing it killed me.

I gave a quick heave, thrust my knee under the raised sack, and jerked it up on to my shoulder, staggering under the weight. Steadying the bag on my shoulder, I took a quick turn up and down the lobby.

'Good life, you are near bursting,' Morag crowed, starting to giggle. 'Your face is as red as a beetroot.'

I slid the bag to the floor, panting, and propped it against the wall. 'Try it,' I said, well pleased with myself. 'You would never get it clear o' the floor.'

'It is easy enough to lift a bag o' meal,' Morag jibed, 'but not so easy to tackle the Factor about a job.'

'Who would blame Niall for that?' Catriona said. 'I don't fancy the look of the new Factor at all. They say he is a terrible cross man, too.'

'Ach, I wouldn't think anything of it,' I said.

'Take no heed of him and his boasting, Catriona,' Morag said. 'He is all talk, just. I bet he would take to his heels the minute he clapped eyes on the Factor.'

'That is where you are wrong, lassie,' I cried, furious with her. 'I am going to see him right now, and ask him for a job at the salmon fishing.'

'Wait . . .' Morag started.

But I did not stop to hear what she had to say. I had heard too much from her already. Slamming the door behind me, I stormed out of the house.

Chapter Three

The Factor stayed in the Big House, the home of the Laird. The Laird had another estate on the mainland, and it must have suited him better than this one, because he hardly ever came near the place. It was a fine house, too, standing on the north bank of the river, close to the shore.

It was well sheltered by trees, and I mind my father telling me that when he was a boy there was an army of gardeners and gamekeepers employed about the place. My father said they were on the go all the time. Not even a falling leaf was allowed to lie on the paths for more than a minute or two, and there were swarms of them patrolling the river in case a poor crofter might try to poach a salmon.

But it was changed days now, only the one gardener, and him an old man near done, and one gamekeeper. Not that the estate was in a bad way, mind you. The Laird had the rents from all the crofts, and everyone said he was making a fortune at the salmon fishing.

The gardener and the gamekeeper stayed in cottages in the grounds. The Factor had the Big House all to himself, except for his housekeeper, and two girls who worked in the wing that was used as the estate office.

By the time I had reached the footbridge across the river, my anger – and a good deal of my courage – had left me. For all my boasting, I was not keen on tackling the new Factor, as Morag knew only too well. For one thing, he was an Englishman, and he had a queer tongue on him, quick and clipped, biting the words off before they were hardly out of his mouth. He had spoken to me at the last Rent Collection, and I had not made out but one word in ten.

I leaned over the rail of the footbridge, looking down at the quick flowing river as it hurried to meet the sea. The water swirling under the bridge, and hustling down the rock-strewn channel, put me in mind of the new Factor. Everything about him was hurried, as if an unseen figure was poking him in the back with a stick, and hissing in his ear: 'Be quick now! Be quick!'

He was not a bit like the old Factor, who was slow and easy and a great talker. It was said of him that he would take half the day to fill his pipe, once he had settled down for a right crack. Oh, he was a lovely man for talk, the old Factor.

He would stand back and squint at you, and stroke his chin and say: 'Now, let me see, I just can't mind the name.' And when you made to speak he would hold up his hand and put on a terrible frown, and say: 'No, no. A minute now. Let me think.'

And he would start off with the name of your grandfather (yes, your grandfather!) and go on to your uncles, saying that you had a look of this one, and the way your ears stuck out put him in mind of that one, and when he had spoken of four or five of them he would come to your father, and finally, as if he had not known it all the time, he would roll your own name off his tongue, using the long patronymic, the way it is always done in the Gaelic.

Then he would let out a great bellow of laughter, and clap you on the back, and ask what was doing, and get out his pipe, the one with the bend in the stem, and let you talk for a while.

I believe it was the thought of the old Factor, and how easy it was to talk to him in the Gaelic that made me loiter on the footbridge. Ever since I had left school, over a year ago, I had hardly ever spoken English, and I was afraid of getting flustered and making a fool of myself, because it is a tongue I am not handy at.

But I would make a bigger fool of myself if I went back to the house and confessed to Morag that I had been afraid to tackle the new Factor. So I left the bridge, and took the winding path to the Big House, although my feet were all for marching in the opposite direction.

The Factor was writing at his big desk in the huge room that he used as an office. I felt awkward marching across the good carpet in my tackety boots, and wild with myself for not changing into my good clothes. My mother would have something to say if she heard that I had been before him without bothering to put on a collar and tie.

I stopped in front of his desk, but he went on writing steadily, without looking up. Suddenly, he laid his pen aside, and glanced up at me. 'Yes?' he said.

I waited for him to go on, thinking he was sure to ask after Ruairidh, or maybe start off with talk about the weather, seeing it was the best day we had seen in weeks. But he just sat there, not saying a word, making an arch of his fingers, and tapping them together.

'I was wanting a start at the fishing,' I blurted out. 'In Ruairidh's place.'

He frowned. 'In whose place?'

'Ruairidh's,' I said. 'My brother. He got hurt.'

'Ah, yes,' he said, picking up his pen and fiddling with it, 'I rather expected a visit from a member of that unfortunate young man's family.' He had looked sour enough at the start, but now his face got even longer. 'Some of your legally minded friends, I suppose, have been urging you to claim compensation on your brother's behalf?'

34

'I don't understand,' I said, and in truth, I did not.

'You understand, I take it, that your brother is dangerously ill,' he said, sharply, 'and that this – er – deplorable
accident might well prove fatal?'

I nodded, not following the half of what he had said, but
knowing by the tone of his voice that he was far from
pleased.

'You understand that your brother fell from the footbridge that crossed the gorge above the salmon fishing
station?' he went on.

I nodded again.

'What you may not understand is what he was doing on
the bridge at the time of the accident.'

I had been listening carefully, and I got that all right. 'I
know fine,' I said. 'Ruairidh was going up to the road to
meet Lipton's van and get cigarettes.'

'Precisely,' he said, giving a thin smile that had no more
body than a bowl of watery gruel. 'And the footbridge
exists for one purpose, and one purpose only – to enable
the fishermen to proceed to and from their work. At the
time of the accident your brother should have been on
duty at the station. The estate, therefore, as his employer,
can bear no liability for the accident. In short, he has no
claim on the estate, none whatever.'

'No claim?' I echoed stupidly.

'None,' he repeated. 'He left his place of work without
authorization, and the estate will not pay out one penny
piece in compensation.'

It dawned on me at last what he had been getting at.
'Good life, you don't suppose Ruairidh would want paying
for falling off the bridge!' I exclaimed, not caring if he
showed me the door there and then. 'I was not after
coming here for money – well, not that sort of money.'

His eyebrows rose. 'No?'

'No,' I said. 'I came to get a start at the fishing. In
Ruairidh's place.'

'You will forgive me if I didn't take you seriously,' he
said, dropping the pen and pinching his nose between his
forefingers. 'You appear, if I may say so, rather young for

that type of work.'

'I am seventeen,' I said boldly, getting up on the balls of my feet to put an inch or two on my height.

He eyed me thoughtfully. 'Really? You surprise me. I always thought I was rather good at ages, and I would have placed you at sixteen, at the outside.'

'Well, I am strong enough,' I said, flushing. 'And I know about outboards,' I added quickly, recalling that the coble they used at the salmon fishing station had an outboard engine. 'I was working the outboard on my brother's boat since years.'

'Since years?' he said, smiling away to himself, as if he had just heard a topper of a joke for the first time.

I wish he had told me what was funny about working an outboard; nothing that I could see, unless it was himself at the helm in his city suit and fancy waistcoat, and a demon of a northerly swell making the boat roll on her beam ends. I believe I would have laughed then, right enough.

He asked me what township I came from and, when I told him, he said, 'That is a long way from the fishing station.'

'Aye, but I would stay in the bothy,' I said eagerly.

His eyebrows went up again. 'I take it you do not subscribe to the local superstitions about the bothy?' he said, spitting out the words in that queer, clipped tongue of his.

I caught the word 'bothy,' so I said cautiously: 'I don't mind staying at the bothy.'

'You don't sound very confident,' he said, smiling again, 'but it might be worth while giving you a chance to see what the effect would be on the locals, if you stick it. But I dare say you will be running for home after the first night.'

'No fear,' I declared.

'Well, we shall see.' He became brisk and businesslike again. 'Let's see – today is Tuesday. Report to Mr MacGregor at the fishing station tomorrow morning. Eight o'clock. And see you are there sharp on time.'

I stammered my thanks, but he cut me short, saying: 'I hope you realize it would be unfair to the rest of the men if you were to be paid at the full rate. You will start on half pay. If you do well, we will see about a rise later in the season.'

I thanked him again, and fairly danced towards the door, never a thought in my head of the real reason that had started me on this quest for a job at the salmon fishing station. But as my fingers closed around the handle, the sharp voice of the Factor brought it all back to me.

'One thing more,' he said, 'although you should need no warning after what happened to your brother. See you stay at the bothy after your day's work is done. Keep away from the gorge and the bridge. You should know by now that it can be dangerous.'

I said I would, and made my escape, too elated to dwell for long on the possible dangers that might lie ahead.

As I crossed the river, I caught sight of Catriona. She was perched on a jutting rock far above me on the hill-side. I called to her, and waved. She waved back, and ran down to meet me.

'I saw you as soon as you came down the drive from the Big House,' she said breathlessly, 'but I wasn't letting on. I was going to surprise you, if you hadn't spotted me. Good life, Niall, I never thought you would have the nerve for it. Did you really see the Factor?'

'Aye, I saw him,' I said carelessly, striding out along the narrow track that wound up the hillside to the flat stretch of the cliff-top.

Catriona gave a little skip, and hurried to keep up with me. I could see she was near bursting to hear my news, but she was too polite to ask directly. Not like Morag, who had a nose on her the length of your arm, and could not see you out of the room for five minutes without wanting to know where you had been.

'Was he terrible cross?' Catriona wanted to know.

'Ach, he was not so bad,' I said.

'Was he wearing a fancy waistcoat?'

'Aye, a yellow one. It was enough to put your eye out.'

I laughed at the thought of the fancy yellow waistcoat. Catriona joined in, but there was not much heart in her laughter. I decided I had kept her waiting long enough.

I picked up a stone and flung it out over the edge of the cliff. 'I got the job,' I said.

She caught my arm and stopped, facing me, her eyes shining. 'You did not!'

'I did. I start tomorrow.'

'Well!'

She let go of my arm and we walked on, not speaking. That is what I liked best about Catriona, the way she could be quiet – not dour at all – but not having a need to be talking all the time.

After a while she said: 'It will be an awful trail, though, all the way to the fishing station and back every day.'

'No trail for me,' I said. 'I am staying at the bothy.'

She looked at me gravely and said: 'I don't think that is wise, Niall.'

'Why not?' I demanded, my voice sharp, although I did not mean it to be.

'Supposing you find you don't fancy it, and start coming home at night,' she said doubtfully. 'They would all say you were – well, you would never hear the end of it.'

I thought to myself Morag would be in her glory if that happened, and a small, uncertain voice within me said: 'What if it *does* happen? What if the stories are true about the strange noises heard in the night at the bothy? What if you get scared, and have to make off? You would never be able to show your face in the place again.'

Aloud I said: 'If Ruairidh could stay at the bothy, so can I.'

'Well, I wouldn't fancy staying there,' said Catriona, and she shivered, although the sun was beating down, and my shirt was sticking to my back after the steep climb from the river.

'Aye, but you are a girl,' I said.

'Well?'

'Well, no one would expect a girl to do what a man does.'

'Some girls are far tougher than men.'

'Oh, Catriona!'

'Right enough. My sister was telling me that when they have students in watching the operations, it is always the men who are fainting.'

Catriona's sister was a nurse in Glasgow, and Catriona herself was waiting to go away to start her training. It was the only thing we disagreed on, because I could not see for the life of me why she should want to go and stay in a place like Glasgow.

'Don't you believe me?' she said, when I made no move to speak.

'Ach, I dare say it is right enough,' I said, 'but staying in the bothy is not the same as watching some poor cratur being cut up on a table.'

We had reached the green knoll, which marked the parting of our ways. Catriona's croft lay directly below us, and I could just make out the stack of our own house in the next township.

I flung myself down on the close-cropped turf, shielding my eyes from the sun. Catriona sat down beside me, hugging her knees with her arms, her head bent. She suddenly tossed back her fair plaits and said: 'Niall, why are you so keen to stay in the bothy? It would be easy enough for you to cycle to the fishing every day.'

I wondered if I should tell her everything that I knew and suspected; my chase after the thief at the hospital; the strange entries in Ruairidh's diary; my belief that Ruairidh of the cat-like tread could never have fallen from the bridge unless . . . Unless what?

The foxy face of the red fellow became lodged in my mind's eye, and I heard again Big Willie telling the story of how the accident had happened. He had been in his bunk at the time, and Long John, as he called him, must have been outside the bothy. But where was the red fellow when Ruairidh fell from the bridge?

Catriona had a good head on her. She might see something that I had missed, might even solve the mystery of the queer jumble of numbers that had plagued me ever since I had clapped eyes on them. But I decided to hold my tongue until I could show her the diary, and I wished now that I had not slipped it back into the oven.

'Well, why are you so keen on staying in the bothy?' she demanded again.

'Ach, I just fancy staying there,' I said.

'Like Ruairidh?'

'Aye, like Ruairidh,' I said unsuspectingly. 'He is the only man belonging to this place who has ever stayed a night in the old bothy since years back.'

'I knew it,' she said, looking at me as if I had done her an injury.

'Knew what?'

'Will you never learn sense?' she said fiercely. 'Why must you always be wanting to walk in Ruairidh's tracks? Just because Ruairidh does a thing, why must you have to do it, too? Good life, you are not his shadow. If Ruairidh leapt off the cliff, would you make over after him?'

'Oh, aye,' I said, trying not to be angry. 'I would be hard on his heels just. We are clean gone the pair of us.'

'I shouldn't wonder,' she said, 'the way you talk.' She plucked a blade of grass and started shredding it. 'Don't you see, Niall?' she said earnestly. 'Ruairidh is a grown man. Everyone knows he is wild, too. And he is twice the size of you.'

I propped myself up on an elbow and scowled at her. 'What has size got to do with it?' I demanded. 'Anyway, I am not a full grown man – not yet.'

'Ach, what is the use?' Catriona sighed. 'You would never listen to me.'

I pretended that I had not heard her, and we sat side by side in a stony silence. I was wild at Catriona. It was not like her to speak in such a fashion. If I had closed my eyes, I could have believed it was Morag who was laying off at me. I calmed down then. Of course! I might have guessed, the moment I saw her waiting for me on the hillside beyond the river. That was Morag's work. It would be her idea to get Catriona to try to talk me out of going to the salmon fishing. Well, she could save her breath. Not that I blamed her for trying to do my sister's bidding. It was Morag I would settle with through time.

'Catriona,' I said mildly, not wanting the keep the quarrel going.

'What?' she said, looking straight ahead.

I said the first thing that came into my head. 'Have you ever heard of a place called Morgana?'

She shook her head, but when I did not speak she looked round at me. 'Why?'

'I just wondered.'

'How do you spell it?'

'M-o-r-g-a-n-a.'

'Morgana,' she said slowly. 'Morgana. Wait now, I believe I have it. Not a place, though. Morgana was supposed to be a sister of King Arthur.'

'Ach, that is of no use to me,' I said.

'Well, King Arthur had a sister called Morgana.'

'Maybe he did, but it is not the Knights of the Round Table I am interested in,' I said.

I could see she was not too pleased with me, for all we were speaking again, and she soon got to her feet. 'Well, when will we be seeing you?' she said, in an off-hand sort of way.

'I don't know,' I said. 'I shall be staying at the bothy. I know, why don't you meet me above the gorge on Sunday? You could sneak out the back after church. Nobody would see you.'

She toed the grass with her sandal, and I could see she was going to shake her head, so I said quickly: 'Morag will be going, to tell me how Ruairidh is.'

'How do you know?' she said. 'You haven't asked her yet.'

'She will have to come,' I said, 'that is all there is about it. I must have news of Ruairidh.'

'You can go home yourself on the Saturday, easy enough.'

I hesitated. 'Look, Catriona,' I said. 'I will have to stay at the bothy – on the Sabbath, too. There is something queer going on there, something that Ruairidh was mixed up in.' I swallowed, and plunged on. 'Did you not think it was strange the same fellow falling off a bridge and him so sure on his feet?'

'Aye, I wondered,' she admitted.

'Well, then, that is why I must stay at the bothy. I will meet you and Morag at the top of the gorge on Sunday. But don't come down to the bothy, mind.'

She plied me with questions, but I fended them off, and before I left her I got her to promise that she would not breathe a word to Morag.

As soon as I got back to the house, I told Morag she was to meet me at the gorge on Sunday with Catriona, but she was too busy firing questions at me about my talk with the Factor to pay any heed. When she ran out of breath, I told her a second time, and she agreed to go with Catriona.

Ruairidh's green diary was lying on the kitchen table. I was reaching out for it when Morag said: 'I had a visit from the Insurance man.'

My mother paid the Insurance man once a month, and it was less than a week since he had been. I said so to Morag.

'No, not that one,' she said. 'This was another man, a big fellow, not like that pasty-faced cratur who comes every month. He was as brown as a berry.' She giggled. 'Mind you, it was awful funny. I near laughed in his face when he took off his hat. He was bald, see, and his head was as white as a pudding basin. It looked terrible comical with his face so brown. He was a nice man, though.'

'What did he want?' I said.

'He was asking about Ruairidh's accident. He said we would even get money for Ruairidh's clothes that were torn. Isn't that good?'

'I never knew Ruairidh had an insurance,' I said.

'Well, he must have. The man said he would get paid for anything that was spoilt by the water, but I told him there was only a packet of cigarettes and a diary. He laughed like anything when I told him I had the diary in the oven. He said it was the first time he had heard of anyone baking a diary.'

'Did you show it him?' I said.

'Aye, and I gave him the paper to read when I went into the scullery to make tea,' she said proudly. 'The man said it was the best cup he had tasted in weeks.'

I picked up the diary, knowing in my heart that something was wrong. Sure enough, the centre pages were missing. Morag's visitor had gone away with the only real evidence I possessed in his pocket!

Chapter Four

It was something to know that my suspicions had been well founded, but I was wild with myself for not having taken a copy of the entries in Ruairidh's diary. The figures must have been some sort of a code, but without a copy I could never hope to make sense of it, for I could not remember them all.

But all thought of the diary and the stranger who had calmly marched into the house and disappeared with the vital pages was banished by the return of my mother. She looked pale and tired, and little wonder, for her news was bad. Ruairidh was still unconscious. He had never opened his eyes or spoken a single word since arriving at the hospital.

That was bad enough, but worse was to follow. When my mother heard that I had got a start at the salmon fishing, she flatly refused to let me go.

There was some row, I am telling you, the worst I ever remember. I told her that the Factor was doing me a favour, because I was Ruairidh's brother, that it was not everyone who would get the same chance at my age.

'Some favour!' she snorted. 'The man is taking advantage of you just, and you too young and foolish to see it.'

'He is paying me near the same rate as the men,' I protested.

'Aye, and a lot of use the money will be supposing you

have an accident the same as poor Ruairidh.'

I said I would keep away from the bridge, and stay at the bothy when my work was done. She shook her head, saying she would not be at peace even if I was put on a tether every night. I argued and stormed and, finally, pleaded with her. She refused to budge, and Morag, the great clown, just sat there silent, instead of helping me.

The row went on for the best part of the night, and I thought she would never weaken. But in the end, when I least expected it, she suddenly said: 'Ach, well, if you are set upon it, you must go your own road. I only knew one man as stubborn as yourself, Niall, and that was your father.'

I was pleased at the way she said that, as well as for her giving in, and I smiled at her. But she refused to smile back, saying sharply: 'I don't approve, mind. You are too young to be staying away from home.'

'Five miles just,' I said.

'Five miles or fifty, it makes no matter,' she retorted. 'And how are we to get word to you of Ruairidh, tell me that?'

'Big Willie will look in on his way home at night,' I said. 'You can depend on Willie to give me the news.'

Morag had never said a word all this time, but now she weighed in on my side, for a wonder. 'Don't fuss, Mother,' she said. 'We can send messages by Big Willie easy enough. And I will go and see Niall on Friday night, so I can tell you myself how he is faring.' She turned to me. 'But I am not going down to that bothy, mind. You will need to meet me at the top of the gorge.'

I said I would, and at that my mother seemed to be more settled.

I got off the bus in the morning at the top of the gorge. My mother and Morag thought I was foolish not to wait for a lift from Big Willie, who set off for the salmon fishing station at half-past seven every morning on his motor bike. But I had been determined to take the bus, which left an hour earlier. I wanted to have a good look at the place on my own, and I would have left the house

44

willingly at dawn for that.

I watched the red bus moving slowly down the steep hill to the river. It crossed the narrow bridge and started the long climb south on the road to Portree.

From where I was standing it was hard to believe that the cliff face was less than fifty yards from the road. All around lay a waste of flat moor, broken only by a few peat cuttings, and the winding river that had its source in the western hills.

I shouldered my haversack of food and took the track that led through an old quarry and came out on the face of the cliff. I was looking down into the gorge now, a great cut in the rock that started as a narrow cleft where the bridge on the main road spanned the river. The narrow defile swept out into a huge ravine, the towering walls of rock jutting out on either side of a small, sheltered bay where the river ended its long course to the sea.

The river swept under the bridge and plunged into the gorge in a long, straight fall. The roar of the waterfall could be heard from the cliff top. It fell in a torrent of creamy white foam to the pool far below, throwing up clouds of fine spray that hung in the air like a drift of white smoke. From the pool at the foot of the falls, the river flowed through the rocky bed of the ravine to the sea.

The bothy stood on the far bank of the river, looking as if it had grown naturally from the ground. Its low white walls were capped by a black roof of tarred felt, and it looked right somehow to see the coble drawn up on the hand winch, high and dry, a few yards from the door. Some distance behind the bothy, on a flat square of bright green grass, a fishing net hung from a small forest of tall poles. On the seaward side of the drying green there was a smaller building with a tarred felt roof like the bothy.

Out in the bay, the sun shimmering on the calm sea, I could see the marker buoys of one of the bag nets lifting idly on the gentle swell, and the long line of the cork floats of the leader net thrusting out in a straight line to the shore. There was a sudden movement in the water, a gleam

of silver and sun-shot spray, and a little splash as a leaping salmon went below again. My blood quickened at the
sight of him. I snatched up my haversack and hurried
along the sheep track that criss-crossed the almost sheer
face of the cliff.

There was a thin cover of grass over most of the cliff,
but the track was bare, so that there was either solid rock
underfoot, or a scree of loose gravel. I was wearing gumboots, the soles worn smooth, and I had some job keeping
my feet. Several times I would have slipped and fallen had
I not been able to clutch at the vertical face of the cliff
above.

The track zig-zagged down the cliff face, and I saw with
dismay that it petered out altogether in a sloping shelf of
bare rock, wide enough to take a small hare, perhaps, but
that was about all. At the end of the shelf of rock two
iron bars about eighteen inches apart forked out at an
upward angle over the river. They were bound with
tarred rope, making a sort of catwalk to a narrow plank
bridge that spanned the river. At the other end of the
bridge a rough ladder led down to a massive concrete
block, and there were steps from the block to the ground.

I looked down at the swiftly flowing river, watching it
swirling around the jutting black rocks below the bridge.
Ruairidh must have struck his head on one of those rocks
when he fell. I had been about to move forward, but the
thought put chains on me.

The towering walls of the gorge rose high above me,
so high that I could hardly believe I had descended so far.
Across the river a thin trail of smoke was rising from the
stack of the bothy, but there was no sign of anyone about.
I was doubly glad now that I had come early, so that no
hostile eyes could witness my hesitation at the bridge.

Flattening back against the cliff face, I edged slowly
along the narrow shelf of rock. Once I had got one foot
wedged against the catwalk, I dropped on all fours and
went up it like that. I knelt on the bridge, and stood
slowly upright. It was barely a foot wide, and looking
at the old planks you would never have thought they

could have supported the weight of Big Willie. It was the thought of Big Willie crossing the bridge twice a day that really got me moving, but I did not breathe freely again until I was down the rickety ladder and standing on firm ground again.

The bothy was about thirty yards down-river from the bridge, and I had almost reached it before I realized that a man was watching me. He was leaning against the high prow of the coble, only his head and shoulders visible to me, and I wondered how long he had been standing there.

His face was the colour of old, well-worked leather, the result, I suppose, of years of exposure to wind and weather, and he had the blackest hair I have ever seen on a man. It was the sort of black that you find in a pot of boiling pitch, and there was not a single fleck of grey in it. I thought to myself that he had the face of an old pirate, and I very near gave a gasp when he came out from behind the coble. His left trouser leg was pinned back neatly below the knee, and he walked with a crutch.

He stuck out a leathery brown hand, tattooed with the head of a serpent, the body of the beast disappearing under the sleeve of his navy blue jersey. The jaws of the serpent were open, and its long tongue reached out to his forefinger.

'John MacGregor,' he barked. 'Who are you?'

'Ruairidh's brother,' I said, taking his hand.

He squeezed my fingers until the bones near cracked. 'A good worker, Ruairidh,' he said, and I discovered later that this was the highest praise he had for any man. 'How is he?'

'Still unconscious,' I said.

He frowned and spat. 'Not so good. But Ruairidh is a hardy lad. I doubt we haven't seen the last of him yet. Fellows like Ruairidh don't die easy.' He gripped my shoulder, propelling me before him. 'Away in, and we will take a bite and hear your crack.'

I blinked, coming out of the bright sunshine into the dim bothy, and stumbled on the uneven stone floor. There was only one small window in the massive walls, and the spiders had been working on it for years by the look of it. A table stood against the back wall with a wooden form in front of it, and a huge cork float, like the bole of a tree, at one end. A partition of rough wooden boards cut off the sleeping quarters, and there was an open stone fireplace in the gable end. Sausages were sizzling in an enormous frying pan, the biggest I had ever seen, and a blackened kettle was propped on the side of the hearth, puffing steam.

Long John saw me looking around. 'It is a bit rough, eh?' he said. 'Not like home, I'll be bound. But you must take us as you find us.'

'It is fine,' I said, and so it was, with the rich smell of tar all around and the salt tang of the sea, and outside the open door the river flowing past.

I did not want to keep looking at him, but every time he turned his back on me my eyes went to his crutch. You would have thought that wooden crutch was a part of the man. I never saw the like of it. He moved around the uneven floor of the bothy far more swiftly than many a man with two good legs could ever have done.

I told him I had taken breakfast, but he brushed my objections aside, and put a plate of sausages and egg before me. When he picked up the kettle – and I could hardly credit how he managed to bend so easily without ever losing his balance – he said: 'No fancy ideas here. We just dump the tea in the kettle, but it makes a rare brew.'

He sat down on the cork float at the end of the table, the crutch propped against his side, and waved me on. 'Eat up, boy. You will be a poor cratur, if you don't take your food. And don't be making a stranger of yourself.'

He never spoke the whole time he was eating, except to jab his fork at me, and urge me to take more. I suppose it came from a lifetime at sea in small boats, snatching a meal whenever the chance offered, and getting it down as quickly as possible. At any rate, he had finished before I was half-way through mine.

When he had finished, he pushed his plate aside, and

wiped his mouth, and got out a short-stemmed pipe. I watched him slicing neat rolls of tobacco from a thick coil of black twist, and wondered how I would tell him that I was here as a member of his crew.

'So you asked the Factor to take you on in place of Ruairidh,' he said, grinding the tobacco between his hands. 'Good for yourself, boy.'

I stared at him, gulped down the food in my mouth, and spluttered: 'But how did you know?'

'The Factor sent the keeper down with a note last night,' he said, tapping his pipe on the floor and blowing down it. He looked at me slyly. 'But he didn't tell me you were a boy not long out o' school.'

'I am near seventeen,' I said hotly, feeling the colour rising in my cheeks.

'Take it calm now,' he said mildly. 'I can see there is more than a streak of your brother in you, and that is a good sign by any reckoning. But what do you know about this job?'

'I was never at it before,' I said, 'but I can learn.'

'Have you ever handled an outboard?'

'Aye. Ruairidh has one on his boat.'

'Good enough,' he said, puffing at his pipe. 'You can work the outboard on the coble, and we will see how you shape.' He picked up his crutch and thudded it back against the flimsy partition door. 'Hey, Murdo!' he roared. 'Time you were out o' that bunk, man. There is a new mate here, and he says he can't wait to clap eyes on you.' He winked at me.

There was a growl from the other side of the partition, and a loud yawn. Murdo the Harris man appeared, blinking blearily, a towel draped over his shoulder. He grunted at me and went off to the river to wash.

'They say there are no trees in Harris,' said Long John, 'and I doubt there is not much talk either, if that fellow is anything to go by.'

But the red fellow could talk when it suited him, as I was to hear for myself before I was much older. I was sweeping out the bothy at the time, and the rest of them, including Big Willie, who had arrived just before eight o'clock, were preparing the gear for the morning's fishing.

Long John had gone to the store shed, and Big Willie and the red fellow passed the open door of the bothy carrying a clean net on a handbarrow. They stowed the heavy net in the stern of the coble, and made to take up the handbarrow again. The red fellow spat on his hands, and glanced around quickly. He did not see me standing in the deep doorway of the bothy, and I heard him say softly to Willie: 'We would be better off hawking a pack from door to door, like any poor tinker. What with a cripple for skipper, and a boy near fresh from the cradle, you and I are carrying this job on our backs just.'

Big Willie muttered something that I could not catch, and the red fellow snapped: 'Aye, but we are doing more than our fair share. It was bad enough carrying one passenger, but now there are two of them, and for my part I would rather another cripple than a useless young cratur not the height of a herring barrel.'

My ears were fairly burning, but I noticed that the bold talk stopped, like a tap being shut off, the moment Long John hove into sight. The skipper was dragging an empty fish box, and he tossed it into the coble on top of the six already stowed aboard.

He took the brake off the winch and slackened the cable, so that Willie could free the rope sling from the seat and rowlock pins of the coble. Then we gathered up the greased rollers, placing them under the stern, and at intervals of a few feet down to the water's edge.

We took up position, two on each side, and Long John called: 'Right then, boys. Hup!' And every time he called 'Hup!' we strained forward, dragging the heavy coble across the rollers to the river. We kept at it until only the bows remained grounded, and the stern was swinging idly with the tide.

Big Willie and the red fellow went off to the store shed. Long John propped himself against the bow of the coble and pulled on his yellow oilskin smock. All the men wore rubber thigh boots and yellow oilskin smocks, but I had to make do with my own short gumboots and black oilskin coat, because the ones they offered me were far too big.

Long John swung nimbly aboard, and settled down in the stern. The shed door slammed shut, and I saw the other two coming back to the coble, Big Willie shouldering the outboard engine. I wondered what the red fellow had been saying to him; nothing pleasant, if the black scowl on his face was anything to go by. He motioned me aboard, holding up the outboard without a word. I carted it back to the stern, and the two of them pushed off, wading out with the coble.

When they had swung her round, so that she was facing out to sea, they clambered aboard, taking up the long oars and poling out into deeper water. Long John lowered the outboard over the stern, quickly tightening the clamps that held it in position. He started the engine on the first pull, and we moved down-river to the sea.

Big Willie and the red fellow were sitting in the bow, their heads close together, for all the world like two gossiping old wives busy taking their neighbours to pieces. The glare of the sun on the water was hard on the eyes, so I looked back at our wake.

I could see the length of the gorge to the waterfall at its head, the bridge on the main road looking like a toy in the distance. There were sheep grazing on the cliff top, specks of white against the green, and a long plume of smoke from the bothy hovered motionless in the still air. Looking back from the stern of the coble, feeling the movement as the bow lifted against the swell of the incoming tide, it made a sight that I knew would remain with me always.

Some of the grazing sheep, in search of sweeter pasture, had ventured far down the rounded shoulder of the cliff, where it curved out in an overhang on the seaward side of the river. At the fringe of the overhang a thick clump of stunted bushes had somehow managed to take root and flourish. The grass in the shelter of the bushes was a brighter green than the rest. But beyond the bushes the line of the cliff curved inwards, and then fell in an almost vertical drop to the sea.

The leader of the grazing sheep moved steadily closer to the bushes. I was watching it closely, thinking to myself, someone is going to lose a good beast if it reaches too far over the lip of the overhang and the edge crumbles. I tried willing it to go back, but the foolish beast kept on its way. It was then that I thought I saw a movement in the heart of the bushes.

I have good eyes, and although they never failed me yet, I doubted them at that moment. I should have known better. The sheep had stopped in its tracks, head lifted, staring at the bushes. It swung round and trotted away, joining its fellows on the higher slopes.

I felt Long John's elbows in my ribs. He pointed to the distant marker buoys of the southernmost net. 'We will make for the South net,' he said, and then, as casually as if he were offering me another sausage: 'Here! Take the helm.'

As my fingers closed around the rubber grip, I cast a quick glance back at the clump of bushes on the cliff. Something flashed there, as if the rays of the sun had lighted on a piece of glass.

I was doubly certain now that my eyes had not deceived me. Someone was hidden in the thick clump of bushes on the cliff face; someone who had a pair of glasses trained on the coble.

Chapter Five

Long John's elbow prodded me again, and there was more force to it this time. 'Eyes for'ard,' he commanded. 'All you will gain by looking astern, boy, is plenty trouble ahead.'

I nodded, more than a little shamefaced at having been found wanting so soon after taking over. But I could not remain downcast for long, such was my bursting pride at having been given the helm.

The hidden watcher in the bushes no longer loomed large in the forefront of my mind. It was foolish, as Ruairidh was always pointing out, to let my imagination run riot. After all, it might well be a bird-watcher in the bushes; there were plenty of them about at this time of year, and a daft breed at that, who would think nothing of risking their neck if it meant getting a good sight of a nesting bird. As if to prove the wisdom of that, a great black-backed gull rose from the water ahead of us, and went winging strongly to its nest on a low cliff ledge.

I swung the coble round in a slow turn to the south, and opened the throttle, feeling the bow rise as she picked up speed. The red fellow glanced back, and I was sure there was surprise on his face, and a hint of anger, too, when he saw me at the helm. He said something in Big Willie's ear, and laughed loudly.

Long John fumbled under his oilskin smock and dragged out his pipe. He tapped it on the gunwale and blew down the stem. 'Keep her steady at that, Niall,' he said. 'You are doing fine.'

I believe I grew another skin there and then; one that was proof against all the barbs of mocking laughter a man could launch at me. But I was anxious for all my pride; anxious in case I bungled the job, and let him down.

He was busy slicing tobacco and filling his pipe, which was just as well, because I was having some job keeping the coble on a steady course. She had a flat bottom so that she could pass over the nets without fouling them, and this, with her awkward square stern and high bow, made her difficult to handle. And the strong flood tide did not help any.

I chanced a quick glance astern. To my over-anxious eyes our wake had the look of a dog's hind leg, and from then on I concentrated all the more on holding her steady.

Long John was a slow man with a pipe, but he had got it going like a chimney before I had even started to get the right feel of the coble. He must have thought I was doing well enough, though, for he leaned back, puffing placidly at his pipe, never even giving me as much as a sly glance. His friendly silence gave me heart, and encouraged me to speak.

'Do you think we will have a good haul?' I asked him.

He spat over the side, and sniffed the wind, reflecting. 'Aye, we should, seeing the wind is round to the sou' east for a wonder. It has been bad this while back, just steady from the north, and that makes for a strong swell on a shallow shore like this. It is hard on the nets. The swell grinds the leader on the shore, and rips it worse than a seal. And the salmon won't get in.'

'It always beats me how they get into the bag net,' I said.

'Easy enough,' he smiled, 'although it must have taken a smart fellow to work it out in the first place, and there is not a man living who remembers when that was. Ruairidh was telling me your grandfather was at the fishing. Well, the nets we use are the same as they had in your grandfather's day. Nylon ropes now, right enough, but the nets have never changed.'

He pointed to the floats of the leader net ahead, stretching out in a straight line from the shore. 'See the leader there? She is coming right out from the shore to the bag net. Well, when the salmon is making for the river he always follows the line of the coast, close inshore. And the poor fellow is carrying plenty of sea lice, mind. So he comes up against the leader and fairly enjoys himself rubbing against the net to scratch himself free o' the lice. That way he works along the net, and before he knows what has happened to him he has landed in the bag.'

'I wonder who first thought of the idea?' I said.

'Ach, who knows?' he said, waving the tattooed serpent under my nose for me to bear a point or two to the north. 'There is money in salmon, boy – aye, big money – so depend upon it someone would not be slow in finding an easy way to get them out o' the sea.'

'How is it you never hear of salmon getting caught at sea any distance out?' I said.

Long John grinned, and I thought again how like a pirate he was with his lined, swarthy face and jet-black hair. 'Supposing a trawler took up a salmon in her nets,' he said, 'the fish would be down the galley and into the pot before you could blink. Aye, but it is right enough, they are hardly ever caught any distance from the coast.'

'I wonder why,' I said.

He shrugged. 'How is it that a salmon finds its way back to the river where it was born?' he said. 'It would be a wise man who could answer that one.'

'Do you always fish the South net first?' I asked, wondering why we had passed the net that was set beyond the mouth of the river.

'No, but we are changing the net there today,' he said, 'and we might as well get that job done with for a start. That is the worst of it, changing the nets. Easy enough on a good day like this, but a killer just when the weather is bad.'

'How many nets are there?'

'Six all told, and as many miles between them.' He swung round, and pointed astern. 'See the rocks there, away to the north?' Far to the north a jagged reef broke the surface, the wash of the tide foaming around the black rocks. 'That is our last net,' he said, 'lying off the rocks there. Aye, six nets, boy, and a different net to be changed every day. Some job, I am telling you.'

We were close to the South net now. I could see the head pole of the bag thrusting clear of the water, like a pointing finger.

'Easy now,' Long John said. 'We will go alongside from the north, seeing the tide is at the flood. That way the net will keep clear o' the coble. If the tide was on the ebb we would fish her from the south.'

I half closed the throttle, and eased the coble round so that her high prow was pointing to the north of the head pole. Long John moved over to the starboard side, his good leg bent at the knee against the gunwale, the crutch held loosely under his arm. The red fellow took up his position in the bow, and Big Willie came aft on the other side of the skipper.

'Easy, easy,' Long John cautioned me. 'When I give you the sign take in the outboard in case the net fouls the shaft.'

The moment he waved me down, I cut the engine and loosened the holding brackets. Standing up in the stern, I lifted the engine clear of the water and heaved it aboard.

Big Willie and the red fellow had seized the ropes on the head pole, drawing the coble hard alongside the bag net. Long John unlocked the padlock and freed the ropes. As he released the half-hitch knots, the head pole, which acted as a sinker, forcing the net down, sprang clear.

The other two hauled up the dripping side ropes, and the bottom and top of the net came together. Wedging the ropes hard against the gunwale with their knees, they reached out over the side, drawing in the net hand over hand.

The coble heeled over steeply and the sudden movement caught me unawares. I was flung forward, and would have fallen over the side had it not been for Big Willie's broad back. That cured me. I took good care to copy the rest of them, kneeling firmly against the gunwale, and gripping the side as an additional safeguard.

I peered over Big Willie's shoulder, looking in vain for the sight of a fish. All I could see was a confusion of dripping net; to my eyes, a hopeless tangle. The sea was thick with red jellyfish, many of them fast in the mesh of the net.

Long John was jack-knifed over the side, his hands busy at the fish door of the bag net. I saw him seize the cord that held it, and jerk at the slip knot. He fumbled the cord free, and cried: 'Right, boys. Steady! Up with her then. Hup!'

The three of them heaved up the far side of the net they were holding, and for one terrible moment I thought that the coble was going to capsize. But there was no real danger. She was built for the job, and I could see now why she was so broad in the beam.

I clung to the side, watching the net. It seemed to come alive in their hands, and a silvery cascade of fish plummeted into the coble, powerful tails threshing madly.

A moment before all had been quiet; the men working without a word, for none was needed; they knew one another well, and the work even better. But now there was pandemonium in the coble, salmon everywhere, thumping madly against the floorboards, and sending the bilge water flying in all directions.

Long John seemed to be infected by the mad flurry of the struggling fish. He flung himself across to a seat and snatched up a short wooden club. There was a threshing mass of salmon leaping and slithering all around him. He seized one by the tail, and brought the club down hard on the back of its head.

He worked like a madman, snatching at the fish with his left hand and clubbing them with his right. The crutch slid from under his armpit and fell across the seat unheeded. The club rose and fell so fast that I could barely follow its movements, and I was amazed at the way he killed the salmon without drawing blood.

I knew from the times I had poached our own river with Ruairidh how easy it was to miss the right spot at the back of the head, so that the red blood gushed from the salmon before it was finally killed. But not with Long John. No matter how fast he worked, he always found the small spot at the back of the head that meant instant death to the salmon.

The frenzy of noise ebbed away as the club did its deadly work, until there were only two salmon left, splashing about wildly in the stern. I tried to grab one of them, but it gave a quick flick of its strong tail, and my hand slid off the slippery scales. Big Willie caught the two of them, and handed them over to Long John. Thump, thump, went the club, and the salmon were still.

Long John laid down the club and wiped his hands on his oilskin. He saw me watching him, and I suppose my mouth must have been hanging open, for I had never seen a man work so fast in all my life, and him a cripple at that. Some cripple, I thought.

'You have to be quick with the club, boy,' he said, as if reading my thoughts. He looked down almost sadly, at the dead salmon around him, and my word, there were some beauties lying there in the coble, one big monster stretched against Long John's crutch with a girth on him that would near equal his length.

I looked at him, seeing the great head with the curving hook on the lower jaw, and the heavy body, beautiful with the sun making a sheen on the glittering scales. Perhaps he had battled his way from the great deeps of the far north — from Greenland even — in order to get back to the river of his birth. It was sad to think of him being trapped and killed within sight of the fresh water he had crossed distant oceans to reach.

'Aye, you have got to be quick,' Long John repeated, 'before they damage themselves in the boat. I mind one fellow I worked for years since. He used to run up and down the shore shouting: 'Easy with those fish, lads. Every scale is worth a sixpence to me.' He was right enough, too. They mark easy, and a fish that has shed a lot of scales won't fetch the top price in the south. And that would not please the Laird.'

Big Willie took the covers off two of the fish boxes, and Long John started to pack them carefully, counting aloud as he did so. He handled them as if they were made of frail china, and might break in his hands, and I noticed that he held up every fish to examine it before laying it in the box.

'Eighteen grilse and seven salmon,' he said, as the last one went in. 'A good fishing, boys. I believe our new mate is after bringing us luck, eh?'

Big Willie said gruffly: 'Well, we could be doing with it,' and said it a shade dourly, to my mind, but the red fellow simply grunted and spat over the side. You could tell what he was thinking without needing to be much of a mind reader.

Long John hitched up his smock, and took out a tattered notebook and a stub of pencil.

'How can you tell a grilse from a salmon?' I asked him, as he marked down the numbers.

'Ach, you get to know the difference through time,' he said. 'A grilse is a young salmon that has only spent the one winter at sea. It takes time, boy, before you get the knack of telling them.'

He called to Big Willie, and passed him the boat hook. Willie hooked the head pole out of the water and freed it from the dirty bag net. The pole was thick with slime and he ran his hand down it in the water to clean it, before he brought it aboard. Long John took the head pole from him and fitted it in the clean bag net.

Big Willie took the oars and pulled alongside the dirty bag net until we came to the cleek pole. The cleek pole was taken out and transferred to the clean bag net, and we went back to the point where the leader joined the bag. Willie took the dirty leader out of the bag and slung the end aboard. Long John passed out the end of the clean leader, and Willie fixed it on to the clean bag net. He went for'ard to the bow, and the red fellow got up to join him. Not before time, I thought, seeing he had done nothing but sit and smoke since the fish were landed.

Big Willie and the red fellow started to haul in the dirty leader over the bow, pulling the coble towards the shore as they did so. As the coble moved forward, I helped Long John to pay out the clean leader over the square stern, watching the clean bag net spreading out astern of us with the pull of the tide.

When we reached the shore, the old leader was taken off the land stick, and the clean one tied on. Then we backed out again to the bag net. The cleek pole at the other side was taken out and put in the clean net. We hauled in the dirty bag net, the ropes and cork float thick with green slime, and the mesh tangled with jellyfish.

I tried to pluck the jellyfish out of the mess and got a sting that travelled down my body as far as my boots, and fairly made me hop. I dropped the net and clapped my numbed hand to my side.

'Watch yourself, boy,' Long John said. 'If the sting goes

bad on you, you will be out in a rash for sure, and there is no cure then but to stop the fishing.'

After that I avoided the jellyfish, and the dirty bag net was stowed in the stern without much of a hand from me. The head pole was sunk in the clean net, Big Willie and the red fellow forcing it down, while Long John secured the ropes. He locked the padlock, and, as they let go of the head pole, it bobbed upright in the water.

'Right, Niall,' he said. 'Back to the River net now.'

I stumbled over the dirty bag net, and clamped the outboard in position. The engine fired at the first pull, but I gave her too much throttle and she choked on me. Furious with myself, I hastily re-wound the starter cord, and yanked it back. I was more careful this time, and she started like a bird.

'Another score in the River net, and we are well set for a good day's fishing,' Long John said.

But there were only six salmon in that net, and for the first time that morning the red fellow stopped looking miserable.

It was even worse at the Bay net, where there were only two salmon and a big lythe in the bag. 'Ach, well, the lythe will make a good enough dinner for us,' said Long John, and if he was disappointed he concealed it well.

We went on north for about a mile, and fished a net that was stationed close inshore. We got only seven salmon there. That was bad enough, but worse was to follow. The next net was empty – not a single fish inside the bag!

Long John hung far out over the side of the coble, peering at the leader. It was thick with slime and weed. 'That is the north wind for you,' he said in disgust. 'With a net as dirty as that, what way could you hope to find fish?'

For the first time that day the red fellow let his long face crack into something like a smile. 'I thought the boy was after bringing us luck,' he sneered.

'Time enough yet,' said Long John calmly. 'We have still the Rock net to fish, Murdo. A good net, too. Many a day I have seen a fine fishing there when it was not worth putting out the coble for the rest o' them.'

I had an idea that Long John was talking not from any belief in what he said, but for the sake of contradicting the red fellow. I know that when I set course for the Rock net I was thinking to myself we would be lucky if we laid hands on a dozen salmon. Indeed, from the look of the place I began to doubt if we would see even that.

The Rock net lay to the east of a jutting reef, more than half of which was under water at high tide. The flood tide surged fiercely over the lowest shelf of the reef, washed back exposing the jagged black rocks, and flooded forward again, dashing a shower of spray against the higher rocks.

A group of black cormorants was perched on the highest rock of all in the reef, silent and still as a gathering of church elders at prayer. They never moved when we came alongside the bag net, not even when Long John's triumphant shout rang out over the water: 'Good fishing, boys!'

And good fishing it was. It took all the strength of the four of us to haul in the net, and such was the size of the catch that we had to take it aboard in three separate shots to avoid scaling the fish.

I thought Long John was never going to come to the end of the count, as he packed them away in the fish boxes. 'Thirty-nine and twenty-two,' he cried, as the last one went in, meaning thirty-nine grilse and twenty-two salmon. 'What do you say to that, Murdo?'

But the red fellow was silent, not even a grunt coming out of him. Not that I cared, supposing he never opened his mouth until the crack of doom, it would not put me up or down after taking part in a fishing like that. I started the engine, and swung the coble away from the reef. A harsh croak from a cormorant followed us as we started the long haul back to the river.

Long John took over the helm as we neared the river mouth, for the pull of the tide made it easy enough to land on the rocks at the narrow entrance to the river. As we moved slowly upstream, I saw a girl in a green cardigan step out from the deep doorway of the bothy. It was Morag.

I waved to her, but she just stood there, shielding her

eyes from the sun, not even raising her hand in acknowledgment, let alone waving.

A dozen thoughts chased through my head at the sight
of her, but one black notion remained fast in my mind,
when the rest had gone. My stomach went weak, and my
heart near missed a beat. Ruairidh is dead, I thought.

Chapter Six

The moment the coble grounded, I sprang ashore and raced
up the river bank to Morag.

'What is it?' I gasped.

She stared at me dumbly, her lips quivering. I caught her
by the arm and shook her. 'Is it Ruairidh?' I demanded.

'Aye, it is Ruairidh,' she said. 'They are taking him to
Inverness. He may have to go through an operation.'

The hard knot in my stomach slowly dissolved. I let go
of her arm. 'Good grief, I got some shock when I saw
you,' I said, grinning foolishly. 'I thought something terrible had happened.'

'So it has,' said Morag angrily, 'and you standing there
grinning, clown that you are. Anyone would think you had
just won a prize in a raffle. Do you suppose they would
move Ruairidh to Inverness and him still unconscious,
unless they were desperate just?'

'Is that what they told you when you phoned – that they
were desperate?'

'Of course not,' she said impatiently. 'But they said he
was still unconscious, and they were moving him to Inverness, in case they decided to operate.'

'But Ruairidh has only been unconscious for two days,'
I said. 'When Alastair Campbell ran into the bull on his
motor-bike he lay like a dead thing for ten whole days.
And look at him now! He was tossing the caber at the
Games last year, and he very near took the first prize.'

'To pot with Alastair Campbell,' she retorted. 'Catriona

says they must be desperate about Ruairidh, or they would never chance moving him all that distance, and him still unconscious.'

'Catriona! Good life, what does Catriona know about it?'

'Catriona knows plenty.'

'Away!'

'She does so.'

'Because her sister is a nurse? Is that it?' I snorted. 'Our cousin Duncan is a vet, but how many in the place send for me when their cattle are ailing? Have sense, Morag.'

'I have sense,' she snapped. 'And I am telling you Ruairidh is in a bad way.'

'Aye, I don't doubt it,' I said mildly, not wanting her screeching at me within earshot of the rest of them. 'But it is no use getting into a panic, or our mother will just about go off her head.'

'She is fairly down in the mouth,' Morag admitted.

'Did you let on to her what Catriona said?'

'I am not daft altogether,' she bridled. 'I just said they were taking him to Inverness, so he could get better treatment.'

'Was she upset?'

'Aye, she was.' Morag paused, her toe busy scooping a hollow in the pebbles. 'She was crying. I don't think she believes Ruairidh will ever get well.'

'Ruairidh! Not get well?' I tried to laugh. 'Ach, away! That is a great piece of nonsense.'

'And she says you are to come home.'

'What?'

'She says you are to come back home.'

I glanced at the coble. The men were busy hefting the fish boxes ashore. I took Morag by the arm and led her over to the fresh water spring, well out of earshot of the men.

'I am not coming home,' I said, removing the wooden cover from the spring, and taking up the old syrup tin that served as a bailer. I filled the tin from the shallow spring, and drank deeply. The water was cold and tangy, and it took the brine off my lips. 'I am not coming home,' I repeated.

'I heard you the first time,' she said.

'Well?'

'Mother said I was to take you back with me.'

'I am not coming.'

Morag shrugged. 'Have it your own way. You had better tell her yourself, though. I am not taking anything to do with it.'

'Have a thought, girl,' I protested, seeing the men carting the heavy fish boxes to the store shed. 'I have work here.'

'Well, you better come home later on, once you are clear,' she said.

'Why?'

'Mother says it is not right for you to be working here, and Ruairidh so ill. Everyone in the place will be saying that we have no thought of him, but plenty thought about his wages. They will be saying you have been smart enough in jumping into his boots in case the money might go to another house.'

'Ruairidh would have plenty to say about that, if only he were here,' I said bitterly. 'Good life, am I to sit on my backside at home, with a face on me like a sick calf, to please the old women and their gossip? I don't give that' – and I snapped my fingers under her nose – 'for them and their long tongues. To pot with the whole crowd o' them.'

Morag jerked her head back. 'Please yourself,' she said haughtily. 'But our mother will be wild, I am telling you – really wild.'

'Well, I have to stay here, that is all there is about it.'

She shrugged. 'Please yourself. But don't expect me to be telling lies for you.'

She turned on her heel and hurried away. She had almost reached the bridge before I collected my wits. I raced after her, and caught her when she was half-way up the ladder to the bridge.

'Look, Morag,' I said earnestly, 'there is more to it than just having to work here. There is something queer going on down at the bothy. Ruairidh knew about it. That is how he met with his accident. I have got to stay here, and find out all I can about it.'

She perched on a rung of the ladder, her chin cupped in her hands, regarding me suspiciously. 'How do you mean, "something queer"?' she demanded.

'I don't know for sure,' I said. 'Smuggling, very likely.'

'If you don't know, how did you find out that Ruairidh knew all about it?'

'Because he was putting things down in his diary,' I said. 'In a sort of code.'

'A fine tale!' Morag exclaimed. 'I was looking through his diary this morning, and there is not a thing in it.'

'But there was yesterday,' I said quickly. 'I sneaked the diary out of the oven when you ran out to meet Catriona. There was plenty in it then.'

'I suppose the writing just vanished overnight,' Morag scoffed, making to get up.

I tugged at her skirt until she sat down again. 'Aye, the pages that mattered vanished, right enough,' I said. 'They vanished in the pocket of that fly fellow who told you he was an Insurance man.'

Morag's face was a study. 'You are spinning a tall one,' she accused me.

'I am not. You look at the diary when you get back home. There is a whole month missing, the last week in May, and the best part of June. That fellow who told you he was an Insurance man must have ripped out the pages when you were making tea for him. No wonder he said it was a good cup.'

Morag never said a word, just knitted her brows and scowled, the way she always did when she was thinking deeply. Finally she said: 'If our mother knew about this, she would be down here herself to collect you.'

It was my turn to scowl now. 'There is no danger of that, if you use your head, lassie,' I said sharply. 'Tell her they would be stuck here without me. Tell her I am doing fine. I am, too. I took out the coble by myself this morning. She will soon get used to me being away.'

'She will be wild, though,' Morag warned.

'Ach, she will get over it. See and do as I say now.'

She nodded. 'But how will I know how you are getting on about the smuggling?'

'I don't even know if it is smuggling,' I said impatiently. 'And see you keep a still tongue in your head about it. Not a word, mind.'

'Not even to Catriona?'

I took my time before I spoke, wanting to look as if I had to think over my reply. 'Well, you can speak to Catriona about it, if you like,' I said. 'But not another soul, mind. I will meet you at the top of the gorge on Friday, the way we arranged.'

'And you will tell me all your news?' she said eagerly.

'If I have any,' I said.

Morag glanced down-river. I followed her gaze, seeing the men heaving the dirty nets out of the coble and into the river. 'I would watch my tongue with the Harris man, if I were you,' she said. 'I don't fancy the look of that fellow.'

'Ach, he never comes near me,' I said.

'Well, watch what you say to him.'

'The chance would be nice,' I said.

It is queer how you can say a thing and believe it to be true, and then have something happen that makes a mockery of your words. It was like that when I went back to join the rest of them. The red fellow not only came near me, he was the first one to speak.

He and Big Willie were trampling the dirty nets in the shallows, staining the clear water a dirty brown. Long John was sitting on a flat rock some yards away, gutting the lythe we had caught. When the red fellow saw me coming, he stamped out of the river and stood in my path.

'I saw your sister,' he said gruffly. 'Is it bad news about Ruairidh?'

'No, not bad,' I said, unwilling to admit my fears to him. 'They are moving him to Inverness just.'

'Did he come round yet?' he asked, and I could have sworn that the anxiety in his voice was not faked.

'No, he is still unconscious,' I said.

'Well, well, poor Ruairidh. It is hard lines on him.' He shouted to the other two: 'Ruairidh is still unconscious, poor fellow.'

'The same fellow has a hard head on him, Murdo, remember that,' cried Long John, and there was a sharpness in his voice that was not usually there. He heaved himself upright, and washed the slit lythe in the river.

The red fellow grunted and lumbered off to the bothy. I saw him come out with the kettle and fill it at the spring. Long John chuckled. 'There is no need for a watch on this job,' he said. 'You can tell the time fine by Murdo's stomach.'

I picked up a scrubbing brush and joined Big Willie in the river, and set to work brushing the green slime off the ropes and cork floats of the dirty nets. Big Willie straightened his back, the brush he held almost swallowed in his huge ham of a fist. He looked around. Long John and the red fellow had disappeared inside the bothy.

'The Harris man is not slow at complaining,' he said sourly, 'and he is not slow at making his escape, either, when there is work to be done. Long John could cook the lythe well enough without that idle cratur having his long nose hanging over the pot as if he had not seen food in weeks.'

'Why does he not order him out?' I said.

'Ach, he is too soft with him,' Big Willie muttered. 'Too soft altogether.'

He bent again to his task, and I got down to it along with him. It was a thankless job, scrubbing away at the thick slime on the ropes and the floats, and plucking the tangled weed from the net. I took good care to poke the clinging jellyfish free with the end of the brush, keeping my hands away from them.

When we had got the worst of the dirt off, we dragged the nets up the river bank, and stacked them ready for the barrows. We were coming back from the store shed with two handbarrows, when Long John called from the bothy that dinner was ready.

67

Although I had never let on to Morag, I had been worried stiff by her news. It spoilt my pleasure in the dinner and it was a good dinner, too. We had huge plate-fuls of boiled lythe, and thick slices of bread and butter, washed down by mugs of strong, sweet tea. But all the time I was eating I worried about Ruairidh, thinking to myself that he must be far through when they were mov-ing him from Broadford to Inverness.

I suppose Long John guessed why I was so quiet, and thought he would do his best to take my mind off my troubles. At any rate, once he had got his pipe going after dinner, he started to tease me, saying that I was so quiet I must have left a lassie behind, for sure. He wanted to know when the wedding was coming off, and he said he must have an invitation. Then, when I was an old man, I could boast that a one-legged shipmate had danced a jig at my wedding, and people would come from miles around to hear me tell the story of it.

He was in great form, but I had a job raising a smile in spite of his efforts. I was still worrying about Ruairidh when we started work again.

But as the afternoon wore on, I thought less and less about my brother, and more and more about the tiredness that was taking hold of me. Muscles in my back and thighs, that I did not know I possessed, started to ache, and before long my mind had no thought other than the labour ahead.

We carted the dirty leader net up to the hillside beyond the drying green, and spread it out on the grass to bleach. It took some spreading, what with the weight of the net and the steep slope of the ground. My shoulder was sore where the rope I was hauling on had cut deep into my flesh.

The clean bag net on the dock poles was lowered to the ground and stacked neatly on a handbarrow. A second bag net that had been lying on the drying green was hoisted aloft on the halyards in its place. The finished bag net we had stacked on the handbarrow was carted to the store shed, and we went from there to the beach, where a clean leader net had been left to dry on the stones. The dry leader was rolled and stacked on the barrow, and joined the clean bag net in the store.

By this time, I had seen more than enough of salmon nets, but we were not finished with them yet. The dirty bag net Big Willie and I had been working on before dinner had to be lifted from the river bank, and spread on the grass of the drying green.

I realized then that the sea was the master of the salmon fishing. As fast as we cleaned and dried the nets, the sea dirtied them again, and one bad storm could play havoc with the work of weeks.

When we had finished with the nets, we had to start packing the day's catch in ice, for the boat from Portree called for the fish every Wednesday and Saturday. Back and forwards we plodded, between the store shed and the river, lugging the heavy fish boxes aboard the coble. We were taking the last two boxes down when Long John called that the boat was coming.

She was barely in sight, no more than a small speck in the south, but by the time we had put out in the coble, I was able to make out her covered wheelhouse. She was a converted fishing boat, well suited for the job of transporting the salmon to Portree. From Portree the fish would go by road to Kyle, and then south by passenger train.

The *Kingfisher* hove to, and the crew put out rubber fenders. Long John had taken over the helm, and he brought the coble gently alongside. Big Willie and the red fellow made fast, and Long John hauled himself aboard. He went round to the wheelhouse and I saw him hand a sheet of paper to the man at the wheel. It must have been details of the catch, because I heard the man say: 'Not bad fishing, John.'

The other two members of the crew lowered hooked ropes into the coble, and Big Willie clambered aboard to help them haul up the fish boxes. The red fellow and I worked from the coble, attaching the hooks to the boxes, and guiding them clear of the side.

When the last box had been transferred to the hold of the *Kingfisher*, we took aboard a load of empties and a fresh supply of ice. Big Willie came back aboard with a thump that near shattered the floorboards. Long John stumped out of the wheelhouse, pausing to crack a last joke with the crew, before dropping agilely into the coble.

As we cast off, the tide took us swiftly away from the *Kingfisher*. He motioned me to the helm. I started the engine, and headed for the river mouth, thinking to myself that my first day's work at the fishing was at an end, and I would be well pleased to stretch out on my bunk.

But there were jobs still to be done. The coble had to be secured for the night, and that meant hauling her up on the hand winch; a slow job, and a hard one. Then the empty boxes and the ice and the outboard engine had all to be carted up to the store shed and stowed away. By the time we were done, I could see that Donald Stewart had been right enough when he said that a strong crew was needed for the salmon fishing.

Big Willie stripped off his oilskin smock, and hung it on a nail in the partition wall. He rolled down his thigh boots until they were below the knee, and picked up his coat and bag.

'You are in a hurry, William,' Long John said.

'Well, some people are not able to lie on their backs all night, more's the pity,' said Big Willie sourly, but I think his shaft was directed at the red fellow, not Long John. He glanced around and sniffed. 'Well, then, cheerio, boys.'

I walked with him as far as the bridge, and I asked him if he would call in at home to see if there was any news of Ruairidh.

'Aye, I will do that,' he said, pausing with one hand on the ladder to the bridge. 'But if I were you, boy, I would never stay here tonight.'

'What about Long John and the Harris man?' I said. 'They are here every night.'

'That is not the same at all,' he said, 'and that is where you are going wrong, boy. They do not belong to the place. That is why they are hearing nothing.' He glanced back at the bothy, and there was the nearest thing to fear I had ever seen on his big, dull face.

'One of our own people was drowned here, long ago,' he went on. 'Long, long ago, before the time of your grandfather – and the story goes that he was murdered. It is his cry you will be hearing, if you spend the night in the bothy. Aye, and queer noises, too; noises that would put a grown man to flight, far less a boy o' your size.'

'Ach, I am that tired I could sleep for a week,' I said, 'supposing everyone in the place was letting off fireworks all around me.'

His big hand came down on my shoulder, squeezing it until the bone almost cracked. 'You are not wise making mock of it, boy,' he said angrily. 'The hour will come – for all your bold words – when you will mind what I say. Aye, you will mind, right enough, when you are fleeing up the gorge in the dead o' night; aye, fleeing like the wind, and wishing you had wings on your back.'

It was the longest speech I had ever heard from Big Willie, who was a slow man with the tongue, and it affected me more than I would admit, even to myself. It is strange how the words of a silent man linger long in the mind, whereas the talk of a fellow with a free tongue in his head is forgotten as quickly as a summer shower.

I watched him cross the bridge and start the long climb up the steep face of the cliff, moving first the one way and then the other, as the path doubled back on itself. I was hoping, foolishly perhaps, that he would turn and wave or make some little acknowledgment, to take the sting from the angry words he had hurled at me. But he plodded on, broad shoulders bent forward, never once looking down to the footbridge. I watched him until he seemed to be no bigger than the size of my hand; watched him until he rounded the green shoulder of the towering cliff face, and was gone.

I walked slowly back to the bothy, wondering uneasily if there was any truth in Big Willie's words, half wanting to talk about it with someone, and yet afraid to ask Long John, in case he thought it was all foolish superstition.

The kitchen end of the bothy was empty. The fire had gone out. I looked at the charred pieces of dead driftwood in the old stone fireplace, and the crusts of bread lying on the table amid a litter of plates, thinking to myself that it must have been like this in olden times, at the coming of the Norsemen, when the people had rushed from their homes and fled to the hills at the first sight of the dreaded longboats.

I opened the partition door quietly, and peeped inside. The sleeping quarter was a small, bare room containing two double-tiered wooden bunks. One of them was alongside the partition, and the other filled the gable end. There was a tiny, crooked window set deep in the front wall, and a storm lantern hanging from a beam in the roof, and that was all.

The red fellow was stretched out on the bottom bunk at the far wall, a half-smoked cigarette dangling from his lips. At the sound of the door opening, his head came up with the speed of a leaping salmon breaking water. The long ash from his cigarette spilled across his chest.

'What are you doing spying on me?' he shouted, straining up so that the cords in his neck stood out in a rigid line.

'I was not spying on you,' I protested, taken aback by the fury in his voice.

He fell back on his bunk, brushing the ash from his jersey. 'Well, if you are not spying, you had better stop creeping around like a ghost,' he said harshly.

I made to go, and he cried: 'Wait!'

I turned back, wondering what he wanted with me. He propped himself up on one elbow, and looked around as if to reassure himself that the two of us were alone in the room. To tell the truth, I was glad I was standing in the doorway, for his eyes had a wild gleam to them as they fixed on mine.

'Do you believe in ghosts, boy?' he said softly.

I had taken a step back before I was aware that I had moved at all. When I realized what I had done, I took a cautious step forward again, determined to stand my ground with him.

'Well, do you?' he asked.

I swallowed, and shook my head and said: 'No.'

'Neither did I, boy,' he said, showing his bad teeth in a wide grin. 'Neither did I.'

His wild eyes darted around the room again, and he leaned farther forward until he was hanging half out of the bunk. 'I will let you into a secret, boy,' he said, his voice sinking to a whisper.

I waited for him to go on, but he just stared at me, his mouth hanging open, his tongue playing around his cracked lips, where the sun and salt air had broken the skin. I seemed to have been a long time without drawing breath, and I gave a bit of a gasp. 'What is it?' I said.

'I believe in them now,' he said. 'Oh, yes, I believe in them now, boy.' And he flopped back on the bunk and let out a cackle of wild laughter that fairly froze the blood in my veins.

I was out of the dim bothy, and into the bright light of the June evening, in less time than it takes to snap your fingers. As I rounded the end of the bothy, I could still hear the sound of that terrible laughter. It sapped my frail confidence, and Big Willie's warning came back to me with renewed force.

The sun was shining. The vapour trail of a high-flying aircraft streamed like a white banner across the deep blue of the sky. From the drying green I could hear Long John whistling a gay little tune. There was no outward cause for fear, but I could not rid my mind of the dread thought that the night had still to come. It took the heat from the sun, and the light from the sky, and the courage from my heart.

Chapter Seven

Long John was standing between two of the dock poles, mending a long rip in the side of the hanging net. He stopped whistling when I came up to him, and nodded, but went on plying his needle. He had a swift, practised hand with a needle; the tattooed serpent was no more than a blur of colour as he threaded the twine.

I think he liked mending nets, for he never spoke, giving all his attention to the job. There was something restful about the movements of the needle, and I sensed the deep content he got from the work.

Standing beside him on the drying green, seeing only a part of the black roof of the bothy below, and the jutting stack at the gable end, the red fellow's wild laughter, and Big Willie's dark forebodings began to lose their grip on me. There was the soothing wash of the sea on the shore, the strong, sweet smell of sea and sun rising from the nets, and the swift, sure movement of Long John's needle; all good things enough to hearten any man.

He was using a wide wooden needle, with the green mending twine coiled around the centre prong, and I marvelled at the speed with which he repaired the torn net. When I told him that he was far handier with a needle than any woman I had ever seen, he laughed and said: 'You should see some of the East coasters at the job, boy, then you would say I was only a poor hand. Those boys would mend a rip longer than your arm before you could draw a right breath.'

'What happened to the net?' I asked, fingering the great rent in the strong mesh.

'That was the work of a fly old beggar of a seal,' he said. 'He was fly, I am telling you. Every time we put out in the coble he was away like the wind. We could never get near enough for a go at him with the rifle.' He chuckled. 'But the old fellow is finished feasting on salmon. He has robbed

74

his last net, I doubt.'

'How is that, if you could not get near to shoot him?' I asked.

'Easy enough,' Long John said. 'There is always a way, boy, depend on that. When one road is blocked you must look for another. Well, we tied a sea trout to the outside of the bag. He was a fine little trout, looking as pretty as you please, as he moved with the tide. But there was a knife slit in the trout, and inside the slit there was a grain o' strychnine. That finished the seal, boy – the poison is deadly.'

He did not pause again until he had finished repairing the net. By that time the night air was turning chill, and the dew had started to fall. The northern sky was streaked with red, and a heavy bank of cloud was creeping over the distant hills of the mainland.

'I doubt the wind is for backing to the north again,' Long John said, as we left the drying green. 'We will be in for a stiff blow tomorrow, by the look of it.'

The high walls of the gorge shut out the westering sun, and it was almost dark inside the bothy. I took the kettle out to the spring and swilled out the tea-leaves, and filled it with fresh water. When I came back Long John had kindled the fire and got a good blaze going.

We sat side by side on the wooden form in front of the fire, and had a supper of bread and cheese and scalding hot tea. Long John had prepared the sandwiches, slicing raw onion in with the cheese, and, by golly, it was good. I never saw the like of him for making a feast out of next to nothing.

It was cosy in the bothy with the wood fire burning brightly. The leaping flames cast a warm glow, so that Long John, leaning forward his chin resting on his hand, might have been a figure carved out of a piece of dark old timber. He looked up and laughed, when I asked why the Harris man was not taking supper.

'Murdo is away out,' he said, 'but the same fellow will not be gone for long once the supper is on the go.'

I gave a long yawn and stretched like a cat. 'You will

be tired, boy, after your first day at the fishing,' he said. 'You will need to turn in early.'

'Time enough,' I said drowsily, not wanting to move from the warm glow of the firelight, a dozen questions buzzing in my mind that I knew he was the man to answer. I picked up my mug of tea from the hearth, clasping my hands around the hot enamel. 'I never thanked you yet,' I said, sipping at the tea to cover my shyness. 'I was meaning to ever since I first met you at the coble this morning.'

I have said that he looked like an old pirate, with his lined, brown face, and bold head of jet-black hair, and so he did, never more so than at that moment as he gazed into the leaping flames of the driftwood fire. So my surprise was all the greater when he scrubbed at his chin and looked downright uncomfortable.

'You have nothing to thank me for, boy, nothing at all,' he said, almost shyly.

I had never thought that there might be shyness behind the bold front of him. I was so taken aback that it was a while before I found my voice. 'But you saved Ruairidh,' I said. 'Big Willie told me. I must thank you for that.'

'Ach, that was nothing,' he said gruffly.

'It was plenty,' I said hotly, 'seeing there were two other men on the spot more able than yourself to tackle the job.'

The moment I had spoken I could have bitten off my tongue, for I had seen enough of him already to sense that he was fiercely proud of the fact that his crippled leg was no handicap to him. It may have been the red glow of the firelight, but I was sure there was a sudden rush of angry blood to his face. The brown hand that had been resting idly on the crutch tightened around the wood until the knuckles gleamed white.

He was silent for a long time. I believe he was wrestling with the hurt to his pride, unable to believe that I could have thought of him as a cripple. I wanted to say that the loss of a limb made him more of a man, not less, but that would not have helped any. A wrong word is like a dagger stroke; time alone can heal the wound.

When he spoke at last, there was the touch of a smile on his face. 'Willie was in his bunk when Ruairidh fell,' he said, 'but I was standing at the door of the bothy. So it had to be me, boy. And one leg is near as good as two in the water.'

I should have left well alone at that, but a question that had been boiling up within me for long enough spilled out before I could check my tongue. 'What about the Harris man?' I said.

'What about him?' Long John retorted, his chin resting on the padded crook of the crutch, gazing straight ahead into the fire.

Now that it was spoken and out, I had to go on. 'Well, where was he when Ruairidh fell off the bridge?'

A hand like a steel clamp closed around the back of my neck. I was wrenched off the form and held up like a kicking rabbit. The mug of tea clattered on the stone floor. I tried to twist round, but the grip on my neck tightened. I cried out in pain.

'What is it to you where I was when Ruairidh fell?' the red fellow's voice hissed in my ear.

Long John had hopped up off the form. With my head forced down by the red fellow's powerful arm, I could see only the lower part of his body. The crutch was tapping the floor impatiently, sending up little spurts of dust.

'Take your big paws off the boy, Murdo,' he growled, and I was glad that I could not see his face, for there was a something in his voice I did not like to hear.

The red fellow took no heed, tightening his grip on my neck until I squirmed. 'What is it to you where I was when Ruairidh fell?' he said a second time, his voice thick with rage. When I did not answer, he shook me like a dog with a rat between its teeth.

Through eyes misted with tears of pain, I could see the angry rapping of the crutch on the floor. I tried to twist free, but all I gained was a further shaking.

'Murdo!' Long John's voice rang out sharp as a bugle call. I felt the terrible pressure on my neck ease a little, but the hand still held me fast.

77

'When I had two whole legs they used to say I was a bad fellow to cross,' he said softly. 'You mind them saying that, Murdo? Well, it is worse I have got, not better, ever since they took off my leg and gave me this piece o' useless timber. Useless!' He spat on the floor. 'No bone or muscle or good red blood, curse it. Just a hunk o' useless timber. But I can put it to good use when I am crossed.'

The words were hardly out of his mouth when I saw his hand reach down and toss the crutch in the air. The red fellow must have seen him too, for he released me and stepped back. But he was too late. Long John caught the crutch near the end of the shaft and brought it down across the Harris man's back. He let out a yell of pain and stumbled against the door. It crashed shut against his weight.

Long John had the crutch under his armpit again. He moved forward slowly. I tensed myself, ready to go to his aid, in case the red fellow attacked him. But Murdo cowered back, putting up his arms to shield his head.

'Aye, you might well try to hide that thick head of yours,' Long John sneered. He rapped the crutch on the floor. 'Many a skull was laid open by this timber mate o' mine, Murdo, many a one.' The crutch struck the floor again. 'And I swear I will lay into you with him if I see you put a finger on the boy again.'

The red fellow started to protest, but he got no chance to make a case against me. Long John brought the crutch down across his back with a resounding thwack. 'Away to your bunk, man, and out o' my sight,' he stormed, driving the Harris man before him with quick prods of the crutch, as if he were an obstinate stirk. 'Off with you,' he roared. 'Out you go, you great stot.'

The red fellow backed away. Indeed, it would have taken a bold man to stand his ground, for the crutch was a deadly weapon in the hands of Long John. He followed the Harris man into the other room, and slammed the door with a force that shook the wooden partition.

I went back to the fire, listening anxiously, afraid that a fight would break out between them. But there was no sound of blows being struck. All I could hear was the deep rumble of Long John's voice and an occasional muttered word from the red fellow.

Long John's voice rumbled on and on and on. I thought of Big Willie making out he was too soft, and I wondered what he would say if he could hear the red fellow meekly taking a long lecture. He would not be so free with his own tongue, that much was certain. I tossed a piece of driftwood on to the fire, sending a flurry of sparks up the wide chimney.

Long John came up behind me so quietly that I started at the sudden touch of his hand on my shoulder. 'I believe you were dozing,' he said. 'Did he hurt you?'

'No, he did not,' I said. I rubbed the back of my neck. 'I am a bit stiff just.'

'Come on,' he said. 'We will take a turn to the shore before bed.'

It was dusk, and the high walls of the gorge seemed to shut out the sky. We walked in silence to the shore. The tide had ebbed, laying bare a thin crescent of white sand in the bay.

'I have had it out with Murdo,' Long John said, putting a hand on my shoulder. 'He sees now that he went wrong. I believe he is heart sorry, boy, but he got flaming mad at you. He heard you asking me where he was when Ruairidh fell, and he thought you were making him out a coward. Mind you, he had no right to set about you, none at all, but I can see now why he got wild.'

'I was not making him out a coward,' I said. 'I just wondered where he was when Ruairidh fell off the bridge.'

Long John chuckled, his good humour restored. 'Well you might wonder,' he said, 'and not only on the day of poor Ruairidh's accident. Half the time I never know my-self. If there is work on the go, depend upon it the bold Murdo will make himself scarce.'

'Aye, but there was a gale blowing on Monday,' I persisted. 'You were not able to make out with the coble, mind. So there was no work for him to dodge that day.'

'Well, yes, you are right,' he said thoughtfully. 'You

have a good memory on you, boy.'

'And he was not along with Big Willie,' I plunged on, determined to have it out once and for all.

'No, Willie was in his bunk,' Long John agreed.

'And you were at the door of the bothy,' I said, gradually working round to it.

'Aye, so I was.' He smiled a little. 'It is a morning I am not likely to forget. I was at the door of the bothy, right enough.'

'Did you see Ruairidh fall?' I asked.

'Well, I heard a cry. I believe he was in the river before I spotted him.'

I picked up a flat pebble and sent it skimming out over the water, wondering how I could put into words what I had so clearly in my mind.

Long John said: 'You are biting deep on something, boy. What is it?'

I swallowed. 'It is Ruairidh,' I said. 'He could never have fallen off the bridge. He was too quick on his feet for that.'

Long John drew in a deep breath. I felt his hand tighten on my shoulder. 'Do you think he was pushed, eh? Is that it?'

I nodded, thankful to have got it off my chest without having to put it into words.

'And you think Murdo, the Harris man, is the fellow who pushed him?'

I nodded again.

Long John drew another deep breath. 'What makes you think Murdo would want to see the end of poor Ruairidh?' he asked.

It was on the tip of my tongue to tell him everything, but I was afraid that he would not believe me if I told him the story about the stranger who had called on Morag, and disappeared with the missing pages of Ruairidh's diary. If only I had been able to show him the entries in the diary it would have been different, but without them I was sure he would think I was spinning a tall one. So I only said: 'Who else could have pushed Ruairidh off the bridge?'

'You have it all worked out, eh?' he said, not mocking

me at all, but sounding as if he could hardly believe his ears. 'Oh, the red fellow is not easy to work with, right enough,' he went on. 'He is just a great lazy lump of a cratur, with no more sense in his head than a stot. For all the use he is at the fishing, he might as well be lying on his back in Harris. And the same fellow has a dirty temper on him. Agreed? Good enough.' He took another deep breath. 'So you added all this up and thought about Ruairidh being so smart on his feet, and came out with the idea that Murdo had pushed him off the bridge. Is that it?'

'Well, he must have done,' I said, wondering a shade uneasily what was coming next.

'There is no *must* about it,' Long John thundered. 'Neither Murdo nor anyone else could have pushed Ruairidh off the bridge. I was standing at the door of the bothy, mind, when the accident happened. Do you suppose I have eyes in my head, or not? If there had been a second man on the bridge I must have seen him.'

'I suppose so,' I said doubtfully, unable to believe that all my careful scheming had come to naught.

'Suppose?' he snorted angrily. 'Am I blind just? Good life, boy, I may be without a leg, but I have eyes. Aye, and sharp ones, let me tell you.'

'I believe you,' I said hastily, remembering how he had spotted the *Kingfisher* when she was no more than a tiny speck in the distance. 'It was just that I was so sure Ruairidh would never lose his footing.'

Long John patted my shoulder. 'Aye, but it can happen to the best,' he said. 'I mind once when I was on the road in the States with a travelling circus. We had a fellow on a trapeze – a great hand altogether. He made it look that easy you would have said he could do his act blindfold. One night he missed his grip, and there was no net. He broke his neck.'

'I never knew you had been to America,' I said, 'and in a circus.'

'It was just a job I picked up,' he said. 'I was a bit of a roamer when I had two legs, Niall.' He chuckled. 'You know something? I was getting real wild at you a while back.'

'Wild?' I said, surprised.

'Aye, wild, boy,' he affirmed. 'Near as wild as poor Murdo. I wonder at the nerve of you, making out that you knew more than me, when you had been spinning it all in your head and I had seen the whole thing with my own eyes. Good life, was I not the fellow who hauled poor Ruairidh out of the river?' He chuckled again. 'One thing I will say for you, boy – you have a great imagination.'

I would have taken badly to such a dressing down from most men, but not from him. You felt he was laughing at himself, as well as you, and that took all the sting out of his words.

He shut the bothy door behind us and turned the big key in the lock. The lantern was lit, but the red fellow was hunched under the blankets. He never stirred as we came in, but I doubted if he was asleep.

Long John patted the top tier of the bunks inside the door. 'This is my berth,' he said. 'You can take your choice of the one below me, or the top one there above Murdo.'

I had a fancy for a top bunk, so I took the one above the red fellow. As I watched Long John haul himself up into his berth, I thought how like him it was to pick a top bunk. He would never take the easy way, because he had lost a leg, or admit to himself that he could not move as freely as other men.

I stripped off my jersey and denim trousers and tossed them up on to the bunk. Taking care not to plant my feet on the red fellow, I climbed up into it. The wooden frame creaked and groaned, and the Harris man grunted noisily.

Long John reached across to the lantern. 'Goodnight, Niall,' he said, as he snuffed the light. 'Sleep well.'

'Good-night,' I said, hearing the creaks as he settled himself in his bunk.

The rough grey blankets tickled my skin, but the bunk was comfortable enough. I was so tired I thought I would fall asleep instantly, but I could not rid my mind of the thought that I had been wrong about the red fellow. I gnawed away at it, like a dog at a favourite bone. All sorts of wild fancies paraded themselves, as I tried to reason how Long John could have been mistaken.

In the end I gave it up, but my mind was too active for sleep. It turned to other things. Now that the room was in darkness, all the stories I had heard about the bothy came flooding back into my mind. I lifted my head from the hard pillow, straining my ears at every sound.

An odd cracking noise in the roof started my heart thumping. But it was only the old timbers contracting after the heat of the day. Slowly I settled down. My eyes gradually drooped shut, lulled by the steady wash of the sea on the nearby shore, the heavy breathing of the men in the other bunks, and the distant rumble of the falls. My last conscious thought was a feeling of pride at the thought of Big Willie's face in the morning, when he saw that I had stayed the night.

I awoke with a start. I was sitting up in the bunk, wet with sweat, my heart pounding madly. Slowly, the dream came back to me. I had been drifting idly along the river in a dinghy. Suddenly, it had increased speed, and I was powerless to check it. Before I realized what had happened I had been swept under the bridge, and was poised on the verge of the falls. The roar of the pounding falls was deafening me.

It was a noise like thunder, *and it was still with me*! I clutched the wooden frame of the bunk, my heart beating like a trip-hammer. How long I sat like that, frozen with horror, I do not know; probably no longer than it took my sleep-fuddled brain to clear. Slowly, it dawned upon me that the noise all around was the hammering of a heavy rainstorm on the felt roof above my head.

I flopped back on the bunk, hearing the noise slacken as the shower eased off. The bunk below me started creaking, as the red fellow tossed in his sleep; that, and the snoring of Long John, seemed to me the finest sounds I had ever heard. I pulled the blankets up to my chin, and turned on my side. I was asleep instantly.

The second time I awoke everything was quiet. I wondered at first if it was morning. There was a faint glow of light coming through the tiny window, no more than that from the lightening sky hours before sunrise. From the bunk at the other end of the room, I could hear Long John breathing heavily.

I lay back and shut my eyes again. At that very moment, a terrible cry rang out. It seemed to come from the direction of the river, a high-pitched screech, sobbing away to a long, drawn-out moan.

I was frozen rigid, paralysed with terror. As the sound died away, I threw the blankets aside, and scrambled up on the bunk. Gripping the wooden frame with both hands, I got ready to leap to the floor if the cry came again.

All was quiet. I hung over the side of the bunk, peering down at the red fellow. In the glimmer of light from the window, I could see him humped under the blankets. He was sleeping peacefully, and I thought of Big Willie's words, that only those belonging to the place ever heard the cries. From the other side of the room, Long John's heavy breathing rose and fell as regularly as the wash of the sea.

I licked my dry lips. 'John,' I called softly, not wanting to waken the red fellow, and have him gloat. He made no reply. 'John,' I called again, a little louder this time. 'John MacGregor.'

He muttered something in his sleep and snorted loudly. The slow, steady breathing rose and fell again. I leaned across as far as I could without falling out of the bunk, and I was just on the point of hissing his name for the fourth time, when something squeaked against the window.

I shrank back against the wall, shaking with fright. There was a huge hand against the glass. The fingers were clawing at the window, and they were stained red with blood.

I huddled against the wall, stiff with fear. Tap, tap, tap went the fingers at the window. I shut my eyes tightly, Tap, tap, tap went the fingers at the window.

'John!' I yelled.

There was silence; a deep, deep silence. Long John's bunk creaked as he stirred restlessly. I opened my eyes and chanced a quick glance at the window. The clawing fingers had gone. Long John yawned, and muttered sleepily: 'What is it?'

'I saw a hand,' I cried, my voice squeaking. 'At the window.'

His bunk creaked as he turned over. He yawned again. 'Ach, you are dreaming, boy,' he mumbled. 'Go to sleep.'

I crouched where I was, cold and shivering, never taking my eyes off the window. A sudden gust of wind swept down the gorge, and plucked at the felt roof. I stiffened at the sound of it. The gust spent itself, and all was quiet again. I stayed where I was, my back pressed against the rough stones of the gable end. I stared fixedly at the window, and the window stared back at me, an eerie, glimmering eye in the darkness. Nothing happened.

I crawled back under the blankets, my eyes still fixed on the window. All I could hear was the rapid thump, thump, thump of my heart, and the noisy breathing of Long John. The Harris man slept peacefully. I moistened my dry lips. Gradually my heart steadied to a slower beat. I straightened the disordered blankets, and rubbed my feet together, trying to warm them.

Once again that fearful cry rose from the river. It was much louder this time, and ended in a soughing wail.

I flung the blankets aside and leapt straight out of the bunk, falling forward as I came down and bruising my knees on the stone floor. I hardly felt it. I was up in a flash and through the door to the kitchen. My hands groped wildly for the key. It was only when I had felt over the smooth surface of the lock several times that I realised the key was no longer there. I tugged at the handle. The door would not open.

Half sobbing, I blundered back to the table, feeling around for matches. Seizing the box, I rushed back to the door and fumbled for a match. By its flaring light, I saw that the keyhole was blocked. *The door was locked from the outside.*

I stared at it blankly. The match burned my fingers, and went out. My fingers might have been made of stone. I never felt the flame. Fear had me by the throat. My breath came in panting gasps.

I had seen Long John lock the bothy door and leave the key in the lock. He and the red fellow were sound asleep in their bunks, so who could have moved the key to the outside of the door? It could not be done – not by anything human – that I knew with a dread certainty.

My legs had turned to jelly. It was all I could do to stay on my feet. I was shivering all over, and not from the chill of the stone floor against my bare feet. I clenched my teeth to try to stop them chattering. It was then that I heard the sound of slow, dragging footsteps. The footsteps were coming towards the bothy.

I was rooted to the floor as securely as a post set in concrete. Fear had paralysed my limbs. The slow, dragging footsteps drew nearer. My heart gave a great leap in my breast and I drew upon some slender reserve of courage I did not know I possessed. Mastering my trembling body, I ran back into the other room.

Chapter Eight

'John!' I shouted, as I rushed into the room. 'John MacGregor!'

I think he must have heard me blundering about the kitchen, and have swung down from his bunk before I started to shout his name. At any rate, he was standing upright, reaching out for his crutch, when I raced into the room. My foot caught the end of his crutch, and I went flying headlong. I threw out my hands to save myself, and fell across the red fellow's bed.

I came down with a crash that would have wakened the dead. Half winded, I pushed myself upright and staggered back. I expected the Harris man to leap from his bed in fury, but he never moved. I took a hesitant step forward, and stared down at his bunk. I could hardly believe my eyes.

I could see what looked like a shapeless brown mass where the red fellow's head should have been. There was only a faint glow of light filtering through the tiny window, but I could see the shapeless brown thing clearly enough. I had suffered more than enough shocks already, but that was the worst of them all. If the Devil himself had appeared at that moment, tail and all, I could not have moved an inch.

It took me a long time to come to my senses. Long John was at my side – goodness knows for how long – angrily pouring out a stream of questions before I realized that I was looking at a dummy. The outline of a body under the blankets had been made by stuffing an old sack with a bundle of clothing. It was the open top of the sack, revealed when I had knocked the blankets aside, that had scared me.

Long John was saying: 'Have you taken leave of your senses, boy? It is bad enough waking me without hauling Murdo out of his bed.' He gripped my shoulder, adding in a kindlier tone: 'You have had a nightmare. Away to your bunk now. It will be time for up soon enough.'

I stripped down the blankets and pointed to the dummy. 'It is no nightmare,' I said, my voice choking with fury now that I realized how I had been tricked. 'It is the Harris man. He has been playing tricks on me.'

Long John found the matches and lit the storm lantern. As its warm yellow glow lightened the room, he gazed down at the disordered bed, and then at me. 'Good life, your knees are cut!' he exclaimed. 'And you are shaking like a leaf, boy.' He bent down, prodding the sack. 'What trick has Murdo been playing on you?'

I told him of the cries I had heard, and the hand I had seen at the window, and how I had wakened him, only to be ordered back to sleep. 'But I believe you were not right awake,' I added hastily, not wanting him to feel in the wrong about it.

'Right enough, I hardly mind speaking to you,' he admitted, smoothing his tousled hair. 'I suppose I thought you were having a bad dream. But it was no dream, eh?' He suddenly seized the padded sack and hurled it across the room. 'Now for the bold Murdo,' he said savagely. 'I will put sense into that great stot's head supposing it is the last thing I do.'

He took down the storm lantern and carried it through to the outer door, squinting down at the lock to satisfy himself that the key was on the outside. He tried the door once, and then hammered furiously on it with his crutch. 'Murdo, get the door open, you clown,' he shouted. 'What game is this, trying to scare the boy clean out of his wits. Get the door open, you great gomerel, or you will land back in Harris in pieces. I swear it, as my name is Mac-Gregor.'

The same slow, dragging footsteps I had heard with such terror only a few minutes earlier approached the door once more. But this time they held no fear for me. Indeed, I was looking forward to them drawing near seeing that Long John was standing inside the door with a face on him like thunder.

The key turned in the lock, but before the red fellow could open the door, Long John had flung it back. He held the lantern high, so that the light shone full in the face of the Harris man. Good life, it was as good as a tonic to lay eyes on him. It was all I could do not to burst out laughing in his face.

It took me back to a day two years ago at the school in our township when Hector MacLean crept up on our woodwork master and set off a firework behind him. The woodwork master was stone deaf, poor fellow, and he did not hear the bang at all. But his nose was working well enough. He smelled the cordite, and whipped round on poor Hector before he was half-way back to his bench.

Hector's face was a study, when the teacher caught him, I am telling you. But it was nothing to the face on the red fellow in the light of the lantern. Never, in all my days, had I seen a man look so sheepish.

He ducked his long frame under the low stone lintel,

and shambled into the bothy. Long John seized him by the neck of his jersey. For a moment I thought he was going to strike him, he looked so wild. But he only tugged at his jersey, snapping out a string of angry questions.

'What tricks have you been up to, Murdo? Do you know you near scared the boy out of his wits? What if the Factor gets to hear of it? Aye, and the rest o' the folk in the place. Do you think they would take kindly to it?'

'Ach, it was only a joke,' the red fellow muttered.

'Some joke,' Long John snorted. 'Are you wise, man? You call a blood-stained hand at the window a joke? Good life, if you are at this carry-on in Harris, it is a wonder to me the old wives are not dying by the score. They must have strong hearts on them where you come from.'

The red fellow held out his hands. He had a touch of a broken rash where the jellyfish stings had gone bad on him, but I believe his hands were cleaner than my own. Grinning sheepishly, he pulled an old rubber glove out of his pocket. 'That was the blood-stained hand,' he said. 'I told you, I was having a joke on the boy just. I never thought he would get scared that bad.'

'I was not scared,' I said hotly. 'I had a good idea it was your work. Once I got right awake, I soon found the dummy in your bed.'

'Aye, with the help o' my crutch,' said Long John dryly, and that was the last attention he paid to me.

He turned back to the red fellow, and I am telling you he gave him some lecture. He came out with words as long as your arm, and he fairly lashed them around the Harris man's head. I never heard the like of it. It was still going on when the two of us were back in our bunks, and it did not stop until Long John had got into his own bunk and put out the light.

When he had snuffed the lantern, and was quiet at last, I could have sworn I heard a soft sigh of relief escape from the red fellow. Well, he would leave me alone from now on, that much was certain, and with that satisfying thought in my mind, I fell into a deep, dreamless sleep.

Five minutes later, or so it seemed, I felt my shoulder

being shaken. I opened my eyes, blinking and yawning, to find Long John smiling down at me. 'Good life, boy,' he grinned, 'I thought you had died in the night,' and his words put me in mind of my brother. That was the sort of thing Ruairidh always said, when he had a job waking me.

I struggled into a sitting position, rubbing the sleep out of my eyes. 'Breakfast is on the go, so hop lively,' Long John said.

I dressed quickly, hearing him whistling as he moved about the kitchen. He whistled well, and I recognized the tune right away, which is more than you can say for many a whistler. It was a favourite of mine, *The Whistling Gypsy*, and the gay lilt of it was in tune with the sparkling sunshine outside.

There was a fragrant smell of frying ham in the air, and I was suddenly as hungry as a hunter. I snatched up my towel and soap, and ran to the river to wash.

Long John's prophecy about the weather had gone wrong. The air was still, and the sun blazed down from a cloudless sky. Out in the bay the salmon were jumping, and a flight of solan geese hunted a shoal of mackerel far out in the Sound.

When I teased him about it, he laughed, and said: 'Aye, we are in for a good day, so thank your stars I was wrong. It would be worth a day's pay to make the same mistake more often.'

He was in great form, laughing and joking over breakfast, so that even the red fellow lost the sour look on his face. Not a word was said about the events of the night until Long John spotted Big Willie hurrying down the gorge.

He was leaning against the open door, his pipe going strongly, and he jabbed the stem at each of us in turn. 'Not a word to Big Willie about last night, mind,' he warned. 'If the Factor got to hear about it, I am the one who would get it in the neck for allowing such nonsense.'

We both nodded and no more was said.

I walked up to the bridge to meet Big Willie. The moment I clapped eyes on his face I knew there was no fresh news of Ruairidh. 'Morag is to phone the hospital tonight,' he said, and then, looking at me as if I had sprouted two heads all of a sudden: 'Did you sleep sound, boy.'

'Like a top,' I said, not wanting to lie, but mindful of Long John's warning.

'Well, well,' he said, 'there are bags under your eyes I could near get a grip on. I doubt you were awake the best part o' the night.'

'Well, Long John had some job waking me this morning,' I said hotly, and that was true enough.

Big Willie grunted, and sniffed. 'Wait you,' he declared. 'Time enough for the boasting when you have stayed in the bothy for a week or more.'

I had not been boasting, but I did not argue with him, afraid that he might speak to my mother if I angered him, and urge her to take me away. It was as well that I held my tongue, for he said: 'Your mother is wild at you staying here. But I told her a bad night at the bothy, and a day or two's fishing in dirty weather would soon scunner you.'

He was always a crabbit man first thing in the morning, Big Willie, so I let him rattle on, never heeding a word, but feeling sorry for Mary, Hector the Shoemaker's daughter, who was to marry him in the autumn. Mary had a sharp enough tongue herself. She would just need to steer clear of him until the sun was high in the sky, or there was going to be some racket when the pair of them got together.

Willie dumped his bag in the bothy, and stripped off the old army greatcoat he wore on the motor-bike, and we got the coble ready. The red fellow seemed to have taken his lecture to heart. He bustled around like a new man, rushing to help with the nets, and never once stopping to light a cigarette, so as to dodge his share of a heavy lift. As for Long John, he had a cheery word for us all, cracking away good style, so that even Big Willie had to laugh. And it was a good man who could get a laugh out of Willie before he had taken his dinner.

As the coble nosed downstream into the bright glare of

sun and sea, I thought to myself I would be as happy as a bird if it were not for Ruairidh lying unconscious in a hospital bed. But not even the dark thought of a badly injured brother could dim for long the joy of a new day at the fishing.

All around me were the things I loved best; the towering cliffs, rising sheer from the sea, like the great walls of a giant's castle, the harsh cries of the wheeling gulls, the trilling whistle of the scarlet-billed oyster catchers, the gentle slap-slap of the sea against the coble, and the talk of fishermen. Above all, the talk of fishermen.

I came to think of it as the best day I spent in all my time at the fishing. Indeed, I doubt I will never see a better, no, not even if I top the age of Kenneth the Soldier. Long John's cry of 'Good fishing, boys,' rang out again and again, and we had turned the hundred mark before we came near the last net.

It is a queer thing about the fishing, supposing you were being paid more for a poor catch than a good one, you would not be pleased. There is nothing to equal the joy of a good haul, and, when it is a noble fish like the salmon, you feel a pride that is not there with lesser breeds. Indeed, the salmon spoils you for other fish. You come to despise a lythe, or a cod, or a mackerel, looking down on them as so much offal.

When we had fished the last net there were six full boxes lying in the coble, and a fine array of salmon laid out on top of them as well. Looking across at them, I came near to bursting with the glory of the day. And when Long John let me bring in the coble myself, and I steered her safely up the narrow river mouth, I believe I was fit for tackling a lion single-handed.

It was not until after dinner that the first shadow darkened the day. I was sitting on the deep sill of the window, outside the bothy, idly listening to the low buzz of talk from the men inside, when I suddenly realized how Long John could have been mistaken about the red fellow.

He had said the Harris man was not on the bridge when Ruairidh fell, but he had also said that Ruairidh was in the river before he spotted him. And because Ruairidh had struck the rocks below the bridge, Long John had taken it for granted that he must have slipped from the bridge when he fell.

But I could see now that Ruairidh might not have fallen from the bridge at all.

I was looking across the river to the rough cat-walk at the far side of the bridge. The track doubled back beyond the narrow ledge of rock at the end of the cat-walk. If Ruairidh had been pushed from the track at that point, he would have plunged into the river at the very place where the black rocks broke the surface below the bridge.

The talk of the men inside the bothy was lost on me. The more I thought about my new idea the more convinced I became that I had hit upon the truth at last. If the red fellow had flattened himself down on the track, Long John would never have noticed him, once he rushed to Ruairidh's aid. And the fly fellow could have scuttled back across the bridge before Big Willie had time to get out of his bunk and into the open. Long John, struggling in the river would have no eyes for the bridge. The red fellow would be safely along the river bank by the time Big Willie had lumbered out of the bothy.

All afternoon, as we worked on the nets, I went over it in my mind again and again. The rest of them were in great form after the good fishing, talking away to one another as if there had never been a cross word between them. But I had no ears for their talk; my mind was on more important things. Indeed, I hardly bothered to reply when they tried to include me in the conversation.

We were packing the fish in ice when Big Willie gave me a sly look and nudged Long John. 'I believe the boy had a bad scare last night,' he said. 'I never believed anything could put a stop to his tongue, but the thought of another night at the bothy has fairly silenced him.'

Long John glanced at me sharply, and after that I did my best to look as if I had nothing on my mind, for I did not want him to think that I had let on to Big Willie about the red fellow's tricks. But it was not easy. I was bursting to get the big fellow by himself, and the hours seemed to crawl by. I thought we would never come to the end of the day.

Last night Big Willie had rushed off the moment we were finished, but now he was in no hurry to get on his way. He settled down in the bothy and stayed for tea. By the time the tea was over, he was deep in an argument with Long John about shark fishing.

I listened to talk of harpoon guns, and whether it was better to station them for'ard or aft, and the movement of sharks in northern waters, and the best way to render the liver for oil, and the cost of freight on the barrels, and a dozen other points that I cannot mind now. I would have been pleased enough to hear such talk at any other time, but it drove me to a fury of impatience now that I was anxious to test my idea about Ruairidh on Big Willie.

I got up, and hung about the doorway, wishing that I had a harpoon gun myself, so that I could let fly at him. For a silent man, it was wonderful how Big Willie could keep an argument going just by putting in a word or two here and there, and grunting and sniffing and shaking his big head. Before he finally came out, they had shifted from shark fishing to trapping. There is no knowing what they would have turned to next, if he had not remembered he had a tractor coming for peats at seven o'clock.

I walked to the bridge with him, and said I might as well take a turn to the top of the gorge. He laughed, and said by the time we got to the top I would be jumping on the pillion and making off home with him. I think he believed it, too. He was not very bright, Big Willie.

He pushed me up the ladder ahead of him. I started out across the bridge, feeling it begin to sway as the frail boards took his weight. As I climbed up the track where it swung back from the narrow shelf of rock, I looked down at the river. I was standing directly above the black rocks; a fall from this point, and I could not fail to strike them. My foot slipped, and I would have gone the same way as Ruairidh, if Big Willie had not seized me by the neck of my jersey.

'Watch your step, boy,' he growled, 'or you will be joining Ruairidh quicker than you think.'

I took it carefully after that, keeping my eyes firmly fixed on the track ahead, one hand against the rising face of the cliff. We plodded on in silence, sweating freely under the hot sun, until we came out on top.

Big Willie's motor-bike was parked in the old quarry. He had been carrying his greatcoat, and now he rolled it up, and tied it on the pillion. 'That will make a soft seat for you,' he said, as he straddled the machine.

'Ach, I am not coming,' I said. 'I was only after keeping you company.' He had his foot on the kick start, and I added quickly: 'Willie, where was the Harris man when you were helping Long John out of the river with Ruairidh?'

He plumped down on the saddle, a puzzled look on his big red face. 'Murdo was along with me,' he said slowly. 'It was the two of us pulled them out.'

'Aye, I know,' I said, trying to keep the impatience out of my voice. 'But where did he come from?'

'He was there,' he said stupidly.

'Where?'

'At the river along with me.'

'Aye, but he was not in the bothy with you, was he?'

'Well, no. I was the only one in the bothy. I was in my bunk.'

'And you ran out when you heard Long John yell?' I prompted.

He nodded. 'Aye, but why do you ask, seeing you remember me telling you?'

'Well, where was the red fellow when you ran out of the bothy?' I asked, not heeding his question.

'I never took much heed,' he said. 'I made after Long John when I saw him plunge in the river.'

'Did the red fellow come along from the bridge?' I asked.

'Ach, I have no mind of where he came from,' he said, shaking his head, like a stirk troubled by flies.

'Well, did he come from the shore side?' I persisted.

'No, not from the shore side. I believe he was upstream at the time, right enough. Aye, I mind now. It was the bridge side he came from.' He felt with his boot for the kick start. 'I never knew the like o' you, boy, for the questions.'

'Ach, I was just wondering how it was the Harris man was not in the river before Long John,' I said.

'I wish you would use sense,' Big Willie said, speaking to me as if I were as thick in the head as himself. 'A lot of use he would have been. Murdo is the same as myself. Neither of us can swim a stroke. Besides, Long John was the first to reach the river.'

The engine roared into life at the first kick. I watched him move off, legs hanging loosely over the sides, as the motor-bike bumped slowly over the rough ground.

The long wait for Big Willie had been more than worth while. I had been proved right, in spite of Long John's disbelief. The red fellow had come down from the bridge after all. Without a doubt, it was his hand that had plunged my brother into the river.

For a few minutes I savoured my triumph. But that soon passed. I was only at the start of the road, I told myself. It was one thing to prove to my own satisfaction that the red fellow had tried to kill Ruairidh; it was another matter altogether to get other people to believe me. And that had to be done; either that, or some means found of forcing the Harris man to admit his guilt.

I wandered out of the quarry and on to the main road, lost in thought. I took the road down the steep hill to the bridge, wondering why he had tried to kill Ruairidh. If only I knew what 'Morgana' was, and the numbers that had been written in the diary. That lay at the root of the mystery, but how would I ever solve it? I was still no nearer a solution by the time I reached the bridge.

I leaned over the iron rail of the bridge, watching the falls thundering down the gorge to the pool far below. The pool was hidden in clouds of white spray, and the thick bushes, clinging to the narrow cleft in the rock, hid the rest of the gorge from view.

A deep voice behind me said: 'Impressive sight, isn't it?'

I whirled round, startled, for I had not heard a sound. A big man was standing behind me, smiling widely. I could not help smiling back, for he was a comical-looking sight. He was wearing the fanciest shirt I had ever clapped eyes on. It had short sleeves, and stripes all over it in different colours, and it was so thin I believe you could have spit through it. He had open-toed sandals on his feet, and a sort of jockey cap on his head, a tight-fitting thing with a long, white peak to it. A good-looking pair of brown legs stuck out from a pair of khaki shorts, and that was a wonder, because most of the tourists I see in shorts have legs on them like matchsticks. His face was tanned a deep brown, too, and he had a healthy look about him.

'Sorry if I gave you a start,' he said. 'In my job you get accustomed to moving quietly.' He brushed the midges away from his face. 'You live here, young fellow?'

I nodded.

'Lucky chap,' he said. 'How I envy you.'

He looked like a tourist to me, in that queer get-up, and I asked him if he was on holiday.

'Well, yes – a sort of busman's holiday, you might call it,' he said. 'I am an ornithologist, you know – one of those strange characters who spend a lot of time watching birds.'

I thought how excited I had been, thinking a hidden watcher was spying on the coble from the shelter of the bushes on the cliff face. I was thankful now that I had not let my imagination run away with me.

I asked him was he enjoying his holiday, and he said yes, very much, and then he started questioning me about birds, some of them birds I had never even heard of before. But he seemed a nice enough man, and I did not want to disappoint him, so whenever a name came up that was strange to me, I just nodded, and we got on fine together.

He asked me had I ever seen a golden eagle, and where. Only once, I told him, when I was up in the Quiraing after sheep, and that was true enough. I had got the fright of my life on the hill that day, thinking the eagle was an old man bent over a rock, until he had spread his great wings and soared away.

All the time we were talking, he kept brushing the midges away from his face and slapping at his bare arms and legs. 'I'm afraid I picked a bad place for my camp,' he said. 'The midges are eating me alive.'

'Aye, they are bad down by the river,' I said, looking around, but not seeing any sign of the camp he spoke of, and not wanting to appear too nosy by asking.

'Come on,' he said, scraping away at his face. 'I daresay you could use a glass of squash.'

I followed him across the road and over the smooth, hard ground to the south bank of the river. We came to a thick clump of willow-trees. A small green tent was pitched on the far side of them, and a sports car was parked alongside it. The trees hid the tent and the car from the road. A passer-by would never have spotted them.

'It's a nice, sheltered spot,' he said, 'if it was not for these plaguey midges.'

He threw back the tent flap and beckoned me inside. I sat down on a canvas stool and he got out a bottle of squash and glasses.

There was a camp bed down one side of the tent, and on the other side a canvas wash-basin on a wooden frame, a pressure stove with a draught screen around it, and a neat little shelved cupboard. A pair of powerful binoculars were lying on top of the cupboard. The tent was fitted out better than many a house I had seen.

I told him so when he came back from topping up the glasses with water from a jerrican outside. 'Nothing like being organized,' he said, sitting down on the bed. He raised his glass and smiled. 'Well, cheers.'

I drank deeply from the glass, for I had a terrible thirst on me after the long, hot climb out of the gorge. The stranger took off his cap and scratched his head.

I choked helplessly on my drink.

He got up quickly and took the glass from my hand, as

I was shaken by a spasm of coughing. I coughed and coughed, until the tears came to my eyes.

'Down the wrong way, old chap?' he said sympathetically. 'Too bad.' He looked at the tiny shreds of orange floating in the glass. 'A bit probably stuck in your throat. Nasty, when you get a choking fit.'

I knew well enough what had made me choke, and it was not a shred of orange. It was the sight of his bald head. I could hear Morag's silly chatter, only it did not seem so silly now . . . *He was bald, see, and his head was as white as a pudding basin. It looked terrible comical with his face so brown. He was a nice man, though.*

The stranger standing over me was a nice man, polite and friendly. And the high dome of his bald head stood out against the deep brown of his face as white as any pudding basin. The moment he took off his cap I knew that he was more than a bird-watcher.

I knew at once that he was the strange Insurance man who had visited Morag. The man who had ripped the vital pages out of Ruairidh's diary!

Chapter Nine

'Got rid of it?' he said, when I had stopped spluttering.

I wiped my eyes, and nodded.

'Good.' He was as pleased as if I had handed him a five-pound note. 'Another glass of squash?'

I shook my head.

He emptied his own glass and took the two of them outside and rinsed them with water from the jerrican. A neat man to have about the place, I thought grimly, watching his every move.

I wondered if I should take the chance, when he had his back turned, and run for it. But I decided to stay where I was. If I took to my heels he would know that I had suspected something, and there was no hope of regaining the missing pages from Ruairidh's diary, once he was on his guard.

He came back and put the glasses away in the cupboard. He sat on the bed and lit a cigarette. 'Do you suppose the smoke keeps them away?' he said, brushing at the midges.

'I believe it helps,' I said, finding my voice at last, surprised to hear it sounded normal.

'Do you live near here?' he asked.

I nodded, measuring the distance to the open tent flap. It was no more than a yard, and he was at least twice that distance away from me. I could dive under the flap and be off before he had time to get up from the low bed. I edged forward, ready to leap off the canvas stool at the first sign of danger.

'Are you comfortable?' he said smoothly.

I nodded.

'Can't say I care for stools myself,' he went on. 'I always like to have my back against something,' and he suited the action to his words, leaning back on the bed, propped on one elbow.

I looked down at the close-cropped grass at my feet, the brown earth showing through where his feet had worn a path. The tent must have been pitched here for several days at least. I could feel his eyes on my face. He had pale blue eyes, bright and cold. They did not miss much.

'You remind me of someone,' he said suddenly.

My head came up at that.

He studied the ash on his cigarette and tapped it carefully clear of the bed. 'Have I seen you before, I wonder?'

'Not that I know of,' I said, confident that he would never think of linking me to Morag. She had a nose that looked as if it had been stuck on afterwards.

'Strange,' he mused. 'I have a pretty good memory for faces.'

I had a sudden flash of inspiration. 'Unless you saw me at the salmon fishing,' I said, watching him closely.

He raised his eyebrows, and rubbed his chin thoughtfully. I could swear there was a sudden tenseness about him, although he never moved and his face showed no surprise. 'At the salmon fishing?' he repeated, frowning.

'Aye, at the bothy – down in the gorge yonder,' I said boldly.

'I was never down there,' he said, and I sensed, for certain, that there was something tense and watchful about him, although he did not betray it by so much as a flicker of an eyelid.

'Aye, but I suppose you have seen the place,' I said, glancing at the binoculars on the cupboard. 'When you were at the bird-watching. Maybe you had a sight of me in the glasses when I was taking out the coble?'

'No, I don't think so,' he said slowly, staring at me long and hard. I would have given a lot to have known what was going on behind those pale blue eyes. He had a bold stare on him, and I felt my colour rising. 'Aren't you rather young to be a fisherman?' he said at last.

'This is my first season,' I said.

'Do you stay on the job?' he asked.

I nodded.

'How many men are there?'

I hesitated, but only for a moment, realizing that this was his fly way of making out that he had not been spying on the coble. 'Three, and myself,' I said.

'Do they all stay on the job?'

'No, one of them goes home every night,' I said.

'Wouldn't you like to go home at night?' he said.

I shook my head.

'Why not?'

'I like it at the bothy,' I said.

'Don't you think it might possibly be a little dangerous down there?' he said softly.

I shook my head, too startled to speak, ready to leap to my feet at the first hostile movement he made. But he did not move a finger, only smiled lazily and said: 'It must be rather dangerous staying at the bottom of that great gorge. Think of all the overhanging rock. What if there was a landslide?'

'The bothy is safe enough,' I said scornfully, my courage returning fast. 'There was never a fall near it yet. It has stood there for a long time. Good life, my great grandfather was at the building of it, and that was not yesterday.'

That seemed to amuse him. He laughed loudly, sitting up and slapping his leg. Before I had grasped what he was about, he had shot to his feet and was standing between me and the tent flap. He moved fast for a big man, so fast that he had a hand on my shoulder before I had started to rise from the stool.

'Well, think over my advice,' he said, and there was no laughter in his voice. 'Landslides are nasty things, so it could be dangerous staying down at the bothy. It might be safer for you, if you spent the nights at home, like MacLeod.'

I ducked under his arm, but he made no attempt to stop me, calling out that I was to come again whenever I was passing. I was across the bridge and half way up the hill before it dawned upon me that he had let slip Big Willie's name. *It might be safer for you if you spent the nights at home, like MacLeod*, he had said.

How had he known Willie's name? He was supposed to be a bird watcher, on holiday: a stranger in the place. Aye, and an Insurance man, when he called on Morag, I reminded myself. Had he been speaking to Big Willie? I doubted it. Dour as he was, the big fellow was bound to have told us there was a camper at the river, particularly as he was supposed to be a bird-watcher. Many a time I had heard Big Willie declare that all bird-watchers were off their heads, and if he had spoken to the stranger in the queer shirt and cap he was bound to have made fun of him to the rest of us.

That meant he had heard Big Willie's name from someone else. It did not take much thought to decide who that would be. The red fellow! Who else?'

It was the red fellow who had tried to kill Ruairidh, and the bald-headed stranger who had stolen the pages from his diary, so the two of them must be working together. I could see now why he had picked such a cunning campsite, hidden from prying eyes by the clump of willows. It would be an ideal place for the two of them to meet. If the red fellow took a walk out of the gorge at night, who would think anything of it? The two of them could meet in safety at the hidden tent without the crew at the bothy being any the wiser.

One thought led to another. It was like a jigsaw. The pieces came tumbling into place, and many things that had puzzled me were a puzzle no longer.

No need to wonder now how the stranger had known where to look for Ruairidh's diary: he must have been directed to our house by the red fellow. With Long John and Big Willie standing over him, he would have been unable to go through Ruairidh's pockets for it himself.

It was easy to see why he had tried to scare me away from the bothy with his tricks in the night. He must have been afraid that I would follow him, and discover the meeting place by the willows. When he had failed, his bald-headed partner had tried to frighten me with talk of the danger of landslides. Landslides! I would like to start one – with the pair of them at the bottom.

The path to the quarry was less than a hundred yards ahead. I stopped, and looked back. The stranger was standing on the bridge, watching me, his face shielded by the long, white peak of the jockey cap. He waved to me, as cool as you please, and shouted something. I lifted my hand to him and he turned, as if to make back to his tent.

I went on up the hill, bursting to take another look back, to see if he had gone. But I was afraid that he might look up and catch me watching him. Determined not to give him any grounds for suspicion, I made myself look straight ahead until I had covered fifty paces. When I reached a count of fifty, I deliberately went on to sixty before chancing a quick glance over my shoulder. The bridge was clear. There was no sign of him.

I stopped, scanning the ground between the bridge and the clump of willows. There was no trace of the gleaming white jockey cap. He must have gone straight back to his tent.

I searched the moor to the north and the west. Nothing there but a few scattered groups of grazing black cattle. I looked at the shoulder-high bracken that grew thickly on the slope of the hill to the river, and my mind was made up in an instant. I would wait to see if he left the tent. Then I might have a chance to search for the missing pages of Ruairidh's diary.

With a last glance across the river, I scrambled up the bank at the side of the road and plunged into the enveloping bracken. I crawled through the high bracken on my hands and knees until I reached a point overlooking the clump of willow-trees where the stranger had his camp. I could not see the tent or the car for the curving tail of the arc of willows, but I could not fail to see him the moment he crossed to the river, or the road.

I settled down to wait, lying full-length on my stomach, feeling that at last I was getting close to the heart of the matter. Nothing stirred behind the shelter of the willows. I wriggled forward, parting the fronds of bracken, so that I had a clear view.

A tourist bus went down the hill; noisy in low gear. It stopped on the bridge. The passengers got out, and peered over the bridge at the falls. Snatches of their talk and laughter drifted up to me in my dank hiding-place. They clambered back into the bus, never knowing they had been spied on. I watched the bus climb slowly south, throwing up little puffs of dust behind it.

The sun dropped behind the western hills, and the cold damp earth struck chill at my body. There was no movement from the clump of willows on the south side of the river. I began to wonder if the stranger had gone to bed.

I pricked up my ears at the sound of someone whistling, hearing it softly at first, then ever louder, as the whistler drew nearer. Whoever he was, he was a poor hand at it, flat as could be, no more music in him than an old tin can. As the sound faded, I rose up cautiously in the bracken, and glanced down the road. My heart leapt. I flattened down again quickly, the cold forgotten. It was the red fellow! He was whistling away to himself as he strode down to the bridge.

I expected to see him cross the bridge, and branch off to the hidden tent. But he stopped smack in the middle of it, leaning back against the iron rails. He had his back to the falls, though. His eyes were on the clump of willows. He took out a cigarette and lit it.

I never took my eyes off him for a second. All the time he smoked that cigarette, and he fairly made a meal of it, I watched him like a hawk. Indeed, I thought it must have gone out on him, the time he took to get through it.

Once or twice he looked up in my direction, not that there was any danger of him seeing me; I was too well screened by the bracken for that. Mostly, he gazed straight up-river. But several times he glanced across at the clump of willows, as if he was waiting for the stranger to appear.

When he got to the end of his cigarette, he turned round and tossed it over the bridge. He leaned over the rail and peered down at the falls, like the tourists who had been there before him. I watched his back with growing impatience.

Suddenly he swung round and started back up the hill, without so much as a glance at the site of his partner's camp. He had stopped whistling, but I could hear his dragging steps well enough. I waited until he was well past me before I rose up again in the bracken, to see which way he would go. He turned off the main road at the old quarry, taking the track that led to the cliff-face.

I wondered why he had not gone over to the tent. It was because I had been spying on him, I believe, that I did not see the reason for his caution right away. Donald Stewart had been right about people never seeing what was thrust under their nose. It was like that with me.

Of course, the red fellow knew only too well that I had not returned to the bothy after leaving with Big Willie. He would be afraid that I was hiding somewhere, waiting to follow him. That would account for the way he had gazed around when he was standing on the bridge, and why he had not risked going across to the hidden tent.

I looked down to the willows again, and I got a shock. I

was just in time to see the stranger disappear behind the trees. He had been coming back from the river with a pail of water. I had been so busy thinking about the red fellow, I had neglected to keep my eyes fixed firmly on the camp site.

I stared at the trees, and I had not long to wait before he emerged again. He walked swiftly to the road, crossed the bridge, and started up the hill. He still had the white jockey cap on his head, but he had pulled on a dark red sweater, and a pair of brown trousers. His binoculars hung from a strap around his neck.

He came back up the hill at a cracking pace, and left the road by the track into the old quarry, exactly as the red fellow had done. I had no doubt in my mind that he was off to meet him. The only thing that troubled me was whether I should follow him, and try to overhear their conversation. But I decided to stick to my original idea. I might not get another chance to recover the pages from Ruairidh's diary.

I waited until he was well out of sight before I left my hiding-place, and even then I did not show myself. Bending double, I ran through the bracken towards the river.

When the bracken started to thin, I straightened up, and looked back along the track to the quarry. There was no sign of the stranger, and he was easily enough seen in the white cap and red sweater. I broke out of the bracken, slid down the bank to the road, and ran across the bridge. Now that I was out in the open, I felt about ten feet tall, but the only eyes that saw me were those of grazing cattle above the bridge.

It took me less than a minute to cross the bridge, and reach the shelter of the willow-trees. The car and the tent were exactly as I had last seen them, except that the tent flap was laced to the ground. I tried to yank it up, but it was knotted securely at the bottom, and he had not been sparing with the knots.

My knife was in the pocket of my oilskin down at the bothy, so I went round the side and forced up part of the wall of the tent. It was closely pegged, but I managed to get my head and shoulders under the canvas. I stopped then, realizing that it was too dark inside the tent, with the flap shut, to be able to carry out a search. I wriggled out again, and went back to the flap.

There were enough knots at the bottom of the flap, and well secured ones at that, to hold fast a battleship. I wasted precious time untying them, my fingers fumbling in their haste, although I had no reason to be so nervous. If the stranger had gone to meet the red fellow, I had plenty of time for the job in hand. Plenty of time or no, I was never more pleased in my life than when I got that last knot undone. I ripped open the lacing, and threw back the flap.

I tried the cupboard first. His shaving kit was on the top shelf, and the rest of the cupboard was filled with tinned food and some crockery. Everything was laid out so neatly, it was the work of no more than a minute or two to satisfy myself that there were no papers hidden there.

I looked around wildly, feeling trapped in the small tent, unable to stop myself glancing back again and again at the open flap. I tried to concentrate on the search, staring in turn at the canvas stool, the wash-hand basin, the full pail alongside, and the camp bed. The bed! I got down on my knees and peered under the bed. There was a canvas hold-all lying on its side, pushed back against the wall of the tent. I dragged it out, and fumbled at the zip.

The hold-all contained a change of clothing; shirts, shorts, a sweater, and two vests that looked as if they had been made out of net curtains. He had some queer clothes. I rummaged quickly through them all. No papers there.

I was about to put the hold-all back where I had found it when I spotted a small, flat side pocket. I opened it, and slipped my hand inside, and pulled out a square brown envelope.

There were two photographs inside the envelope. One of them was a small snap, and the other one a much larger photograph. I studied the large one first. It was a head and shoulders shot, a bit blurred, as if the camera was out of focus, but I recognized the face at once. It was the red fellow.

The small snap showed three seamen in a cutter coming alongside a jetty. The red fellow was in the forefront of the group, staring straight at the camera. There was no mistaking his long, surly face even on such a small snap. The man next to him had his back to the camera. He was wearing a reefer jacket, and a peaked cap, and he might well have been the stranger whose tent I was searching. He was certainly about the same build.

But it was the man at the tiller of the cutter whose face I stared at the longest of all, my mouth hanging open in amazement. It was a face I knew as well as my own – the lean, dark face of my brother Ruairidh!

I do not know how long I stared at that photograph, holding it up first this way and then that, to the light from the open flap. All thought of the missing pages from the diary was banished from my mind. There was something uncanny about finding, in a stranger's tent, a photograph of my brother. I was so absorbed in it that I never heard him approach; not even the brushing of his shoulder against the canvas registered on my mind.

I did not come out of my trance until he seized me by the wrist. The photographs slid to the ground. He wrenched me round and I looked up into his triumphant face.

'Got you!' he breathed. 'Well, my lad, it was a case of the watcher watched. Two can play at that game, you know.' He jerked at my wrist. 'Well, what have you got to say for yourself?'

I kept my mouth shut.

'The tent was securely fastened,' he said. 'That makes it a worse offence than walking in through an open flap. I wonder what the police would have to say about it, eh?'

'You had better ask them,' I said defiantly, knowing full well it was the last thing he would do.

'No, I think you and I will have a little chat first,' he said, tightening his grip on my wrist. His sharp eyes wandered to the open hold-all, and the photographs lying on the ground. 'What were you after?'

I kept my mouth shut.

'Get this straight,' he said grimly. 'Before you leave here you are going to talk, and I mean talk. If you think you can ransack my tent, and get away with it, you are mistaken.' He tugged at my wrist. 'Now, what were you after?'

'You know well enough,' I said.

'Perhaps I do,' he said smoothly. 'But I prefer to hear it from your own lips. And don't think you know all the answers. You don't.'

'I know all about Morgana,' I said boldly.

That surprised him. I saw the quick tightening of his mouth, and the sudden doubt in the hard, confident eyes. His grip on my wrist slackened slightly.

When Ruairidh was teaching me boxing, he used to say there was no time to stop and think when you were fighting. It was the fellow who sailed in and took his chances the moment they were offered who always came out on top, he said. Well, I took my chance there and then, and I did not stop to think about it. I kicked him hard on the shin, twisted my wrists free, and darted out of the tent.

I caught my foot in the corner guy rope, and went sprawling, but I was up again the moment my hands touched the ground, and away like a hare.

I ran along the bank of the river with the stranger pounding hard on my heels. He was breathing heavily, but I was not gaining an inch on him. I veered to the left, up the steep bank of the river, and on to the rising moorland that stretched ahead as far as the eye could see.

Once or twice I stumbled, but I never lost my footing, for I was used to rough ground. Bit by bit, I pulled away from him. I chanced another quick look over my shoulder. He was a good twenty yards behind, and tiring fast by the look of him. There is nothing like hard going for finishing a smoker. They might be good enough on the flat, in a short sprint, but a long climb takes the wind out of them in no time.

I scrambled up the face of an old peat bog, and ran on

for all I was worth, ploughing through soft patches of bright green sphagnum moss, leaping narrow streams and moving to higher ground with every yard I covered. When I looked round again, he had stopped. The next time I glanced over my shoulder, he was on his way back to the river.

I kept on running until I was almost spent myself, but I did not stop until I had gained a rise in the ground that commanded the country for miles around. I lay flat on my face, slowly getting my breath back, searching the moor for the tell-tale red sweater and white cap, in case he had doubled back, and was creeping up on me. But there was no glint of red on the brown of the moor, and my strained nerves started to relax.

From where I lay, his camp site was hidden by the high south bank of the river. But I had no doubt that he was back in his tent, nursing his injured shin, and planning revenge. He was a sharp man. He would be wise enough to know that a regiment could go to ground in the moor, far less a boy of my size.

I liked the moor. It held its secrets well. Many a distant forebear of mine had been hunted here by the English red-coats, and untold generations of the men of my blood had been pursued across the moor by the Laird's gamekeepers, but not one of them had ever been caught. The moor was kind to those who knew it well, and there was not a bog or hillock in the many miles of it that I did not know like the back of my hand.

I got to my feet, and set off at a brisk pace, striking out to the west. I headed back to the river in a long curve, reaching it at a point miles upstream from the stranger's camp. There was a ford at the place I had picked, and the ground leading to it was deeply rutted with the hoof marks of cattle.

I crossed the ford, the water little more than ankle deep at this time of year, and moved through a herd of High-land cattle on the far bank. The bull was standing a little apart from the cows. He was a fine-looking beast, with a proud spread of curving horns and a shaggy coat that very near reached the ground. He lifted his head, watching me suspiciously, as I passed close to the cows. He looked a fierce brute, standing there on his short legs, a tangle of hair hanging over his eyes. But I would rather deal with a Highland bull than a Shorthorn any day. For all their wild look they are placid enough beasts, if you do not disturb them.

My first thought was to head north and work my way back to the old quarry in a wide sweep. But what if the stranger and the red fellow were lying in wait for me at the top of the gorge? There was only one way down to the bothy, and I had no fancy to be trapped on that narrow track.

I decided it would be wiser to see if the stranger had gone back to his tent. I would know then who I had to deal with at the gorge. If he had gone back, he would never expect me to risk another look at his camp, so it would be safe enough. And I had a place in mind that would give me good cover.

I followed the course of the winding river until I was less than a mile from the bridge. From then on, I moved carefully, taking advantage of every scrap of cover. But all the time I was working closer to the ruins of an old house that stood high on the north bank overlooking the site of the stranger's camp.

The last half mile I covered in a series of quick rushes, bent almost double. The ruins stood on the highest part of the bank, and there was the river between me and the stranger's tent, but I was taking no chances.

Only the walls of the old house remained standing. The roof gaped open to the sky. I crawled up to the doorway and across the earthen floor. It was littered with fallen roof beams and sheep droppings. Bit by bit I inched up to the hole in the wall where the window had been.

Something struck the back of my neck. I ducked quickly, my heart thumping. But it was only a piece of moss, dislodged by a sudden gust of wind that swept through the shell of the old house. As the gust spent itself, the rain started.

I rose to my feet, and peered out of the hole in the wall. I could see across the river to the south side of the clump of willows, and I could hardly believe my eyes. There was a bare brown patch on the green grass where the tent had been. Of the car, there was no sign. The stranger had vanished.

Chapter Ten

I should have expected it, of course. He was bound to seek safety in flight, once I had escaped from the tent and won my freedom. He would be afraid that I would make straight for the police and tell them everything, not realizing that I knew so little. It was my bluff about Morgana that had rattled him. Until I came out with it, I think he had been enjoying himself, playing a sort of cat-and-mouse game with me.

But now he had struck his camp, and fled in haste, all because of that one word, Morgana. That was proof enough that it lay at the root of the mystery. If the effect on the bold stranger had been so striking, what would happen if I suddenly sprang the word on the red fellow? It might be worth trying.

All these thoughts were passing through my mind as I hurried back to the gorge. The rain had slackened, but the wind was rising, coming in gusty squalls from the north. When I left the shelter of the quarry and emerged on the open cliff top, I caught the full force of it, and a stinging flurry of rain, too.

Far out in the Sound the waves had white crests to them, and the long rollers were pounding in to shore. The breakers boomed against the rocks, flinging clouds of spray high in the air. I ducked my head against the wind and rain, and darted down the winding track to the footbridge.

Once I had rounded the shoulder of the cliff, the high walls of the gorge offered some protection from the wind. I brushed my dripping hair back from my forehead, and stopped suddenly. What a fool I was! I had been career-ing carelessly down the track, head bent, not looking more than a yard or two ahead. Going on like that, I would have been an easy prey for any trap the red fellow had cared to lay.

But I need not have worried. Far below I saw his tall figure stoop out of the bothy. He had the kettle in his hand and he filled it at the spring. He hurried back to the bothy and went inside, without once looking up.

But he looked up quickly enough when I came through the door. He had the *Oban Times* spread out across the table, reading it by the light of the lantern at his elbow. The same light betrayed the surprise on his face when he saw me. He picked up the paper, shielding his face with it.

'Well, well, so it is yourself, boy,' Long John said heartily. He was sitting on the big cork float, busily sharp-ening a wicked-looking knife. It had a straight, slender blade and a short ebony handle. He tested the blade on his thumb and said: 'We thought you were away home for the night along with Big Willie.'

'No, I went for a walk,' I said awkwardly.

He looked at my dripping hair and sodden jersey and trousers. 'You must be keen on walking,' he said dryly, and then with a chuckle: 'I believe I was right enough saying you had a girl at home. There must be a lassie in it, or you would have been back long before this time. Eh, Murdo? What do you say?'

The red fellow grunted, the paper held high in front of his face.

I felt myself getting red. 'No, there is no girl in it,' I said. 'I took a walk just.'

'Some walk,' was the red fellow's sour comment from behind the paper. 'You have been gone since hours. Maybe you went the length of Camas Mor and back.'

Camas Mor was a bay on the other side of the island, well over ten miles away, even as the eagle flies, and I knew he was fishing for information. 'Ach, I just took a turn around,' I said, as carelessly as I could, trying to think of something to say that would force him out from behind the barrier of the paper.

The very thing to sting him came to my mind. 'I was talking to a fellow who was camping by the river,' I went on. 'He is away now though. I doubt he got a fright.'

The paper never moved. 'No wonder he got a fright,' Long John said, and I could have clouted him for butting in, 'seeing there is a full gale threatening. Good life, the poor fellow's tent would have finished up in the Sound before morning. It beats me what they see in this camping business. A scrap o' canvas over your head is a poor berth on a wild night. I would far rather a snug bunk at sea. What do you say, Murdo?'

The red fellow grunted. I wished he would lower the paper, so that I could see his face. But I had to wait until Long John had made the tea and the three of us were taking our supper at the table, before he put the paper aside.

I studied him on the quiet. He looked dour and withdrawn but calm enough. Perhaps he had already known of his partner's flight before I had spoken. In any event, he had hidden behind the paper long enough to get over the shock of my words.

I kept on at him, determined to find out all I could about the time he and Ruairidh had been at sea together. 'I believe you and my brother used to be shipmates,' I said.

He was spreading jam on a slice of bread, and the knife was suddenly still. He shot a quick, suspicious glance at me. 'Aye, so we were,' he said shortly, and went on spreading his bread.

'Was it long since?'

He nodded, gobbling up the bread and jam as if he had not seen a bite in weeks.

'How long since?'

'A while back,' he said, hacking another thick slice off the loaf for himself.

A wild fancy had flitted through my mind the moment I had clapped eyes on the photograph of himself and Ruairidh in the cutter. It came back again now, and refused to be dislodged. Gripped by a mounting excitement I said: 'Was it a sort of salvage job you and Ruairidh were on?'

He took his time replying, working the jam over the bread as if it was a task that required all his attention. 'Aye, it was a sort of salvage job,' he admitted at length, carefully repeating the words I had used, and not adding one more.

The wild fancy was a fancy no longer; it now had the look of a solid fact to me. I took a bite of bread and cheese and chewed on it, for I could not trust my voice at that moment. 'A salvage job in Tobermory Bay?' I asked, when I had emptied my mouth.

The red fellow folded his bread in two and stuffed the greater part of the slice into his mouth in a single bite. His big jaws moved quickly, the rest of the bread was rammed in, and he drained his mug of tea. It was as bad as having a hungry stirk at the table.

'Was it in Tobermory Bay?' I asked again.

He drew the back of his hand across his mouth and worked his tongue around his teeth. 'I heard you,' he said sourly. 'Aye, it was in Tobermory Bay. It was a waste of time. We never found a thing.'

A sudden, powerful gust of wind rattled the roof of the bothy. It whipped through the open door, swirling around our legs and making the lantern flame dance wildly.

'Shut the door, Niall,' Long John said.

I got up and closed the door, hoping that my face did not betray my inner excitement. What had started as no more than a wild fancy had been proved only too true by the red fellow's admission that he had been a shipmate of Ruairidh on the salvage job in Tobermory Bay.

I had a good idea now why he had tried to kill my brother, and why his partner had risked entering our house in search of the diary. If I was right, I would have to be doubly careful, or my own life would not be worth a handful of meal. It made my heart turn over to think what might have happened if I had blurted out the word Morgana to him.

I fiddled with the handle of the door, trying to control the nervous excitement that I felt sure must show in my face. But when I turned round, tensed to meet his gaze, the red fellow was missing. Long John started to laugh when he saw the expression on my face.

'Murdo is off to his bunk,' he said. 'I believe he got tired with all those questions you were asking, boy. The poor fellow is not used to working with his tongue.' He was delighted with his joke. He roared with laughter, chortling: 'Aye, he is tired talking, poor cratur.'

'Good life, he hardly said a dozen words,' I exclaimed, not caring supposing my voice carried to the other side of the partition.

Long John leaned across the table, his chin cupped in his hands. 'Oh, but you are wrong there, boy,' he said solemnly. 'Did you not notice how quiet I was? I was counting Murdo's words. He said thirteen words. Aye, thirteen, at the very least.' He threw back his head, roaring with laughter, and thumping the table with his fist.

'Twelve or thirteen,' I said sourly, 'there is no danger of the same fellow tiring himself talking.'

I hardly said a word after that. Long John must have thought I was almost as bad as the red fellow. Even when he said that he doubted if we would be able to get out to the nets in the morning, and added, getting wild no doubt at my silence, that if we did manage out I would probably get sick and be put off the fishing for life, I hardly bothered to reply. My one thought was to get to bed, and work out what I had discovered about the red fellow.

When Long John finally turned in and put out the lantern, I curled up in my bunk, not heeding the thunder of the breakers on the shore, or the howling gusts of wind that stormed against the felt roof of the bothy. I was busy nursing my thoughts secure in the knowledge that I was at last unravelling the mystery of Morgana.

A year or two ago, Ruairidh had been a member of the crew of a salvage ship, part of an expedition that had set out to try to salvage the wreck of a Spanish galleon in Tobermory Bay on the Island of Mull. The galleon had been sunk in the bay after the defeat by the English of the Spanish Armada, and she was said to carry a cargo of gold bullion and treasure. Of course, that happened centuries ago, and the wreck had long since silted over on the sandy bottom of the bay, so it had to be found before there was any hope of gaining the treasure.

The papers were full of the treasure hunt at the time, but Ruairidh, in his letters home, never mentioned the work, except to say that the food was good, and they could hardly move for the swarms of tourists. When they failed to find the wreck, and gave up the search, Ruairidh made straight for Glasgow, and signed on board another ship. I did not see him again until he came home the following spring.

I remembered that homecoming as well as if it had been last week. He had hardly dumped his bag down on the bench when I got talking about the treasure hunt. He started to tease me, wanting to know if I thought his bag was full of Spanish gold, and I got wild, hating to be thought a stupid schoolboy with nothing in my head but dreams of buried treasure. So I repeated what I had heard the men in our township saying, that the search for the galleon was just a stunt to get plenty of tourists to Tobermory, only making out that this was my own idea.

I could remember Ruairidh's words yet. 'No fear, boy,' he had said. 'The galleon is there, right enough. Maybe the gold is gone – maybe not. Who knows? But the galleon is lying on the bottom of Tobermory Bay as sure as I am sitting on this bench.'

I had plied him with questions, but all I gained was the knowledge that he had taken a turn at the diving, when one of the regular divers went sick, and that only came out because I had been asking questions about the diving gear they used. I kept on at him, but he shook me off, making out it was just a guess on his part. He did admit, though, that he would like to go back to Tobermory one day, when he had enough money for the job, and search for the wrecked galleon himself.

I thought of his words now, lying still in my bunk,

with the noise of the raging wind and sea all around. I thought of Morgana. It was not the sort of name I had ever heard used for a ship, but it had a sort of Spanish sound to it. 'Morgana,' I whispered softly to myself in the darkness. 'Morgana.' It sounded right. 'Morgana.' A sister of King Arthur, Catriona had said. Good life, it only went to show what nonsense you could get from book learning.

Supposing *Morgana* was the name of the wrecked Spanish galleon, the treasure ship of the Armada? Supposing Ruairidh had found something in the silt on the sea-bed, an old timber perhaps, still bearing her name? He might even have discovered the place where she had foundered, and planned to return one day with his own expedition.

Would he have spoken to the red fellow of his plans? I doubted it. But the same man would be fly enough to guess what was going on, if Ruairidh had been a shade careless with his tongue. And he could be more than careless, once his flaming temper was roused. That would account for the red fellow trailing him back to Skye. It would account for him getting a job at the salmon fishing, so that he could be close to Ruairidh. It would account for him trying to kill my brother. The same fellow would not hesitate to do murder, if it meant laying hands on the secret of the Spanish treasure ship.

I recalled how he had hesitated before answering me when I asked him if he was along with Ruairidh in Tobermory Bay, and how he had been quick to add that it was a waste of time, they had found nothing. It was not like him to come out with more than a grunted word or two in reply. He was afraid where my thoughts might lead, and had wanted to throw me off the scent.

But why had Ruairidh written the name Morgana in his diary on three successive Sundays, each time followed by a string of six numbers. Now that I thought about them, the three lots of figures were much alike. Each set of six had started with by far the smallest figure first. Could they have been soundings taken from different points on the shore to the site of the wreck? Yes, they could. My mind leapt on. Or chart markings, meaningless in themselves, but becoming as clear as day once they were fitted to the right chart.

That would be it, very likely. The numbers themselves would be harmless enough without a knowledge of the chart they were taken from. Did the red fellow have that knowledge? It was more than likely that he did.

I lay awake for what seemed like hours, pondering the problem. But my thoughts grew muddled as sleep closed in on me. The sleepier I became the more I began to imagine that I was in a ship's bunk at sea. The noise of the pounding breakers was so close that they seemed to be crashing against the walls of the bothy. The creaking of the beams in the roof sounded like the straining of a ship's timbers against the lifting waves. I tossed and turned, and finally fell into a restless sleep.

I dreamt I was standing on a flag-strewn platform, looking down on a sun-drenched harbour. A small dark man with a pointed black beard took me by the arm and pointed out the great galleon at the head of a vast fleet of warships in the harbour below. Her high poop was crammed with soldiers, their breastplates brightly burnished by the sunlight, and I shaded my eyes to read her name the better. It was inscribed in letters of gold, and I smiled to myself as I spelled it out.

The small dark man gripped my arm tightly. '*Morgana*,' he said. 'The treasure ship of my Armada.'

I awoke in the morning to the sound of rain drumming down on the felt roof of the bothy. Long John's bunk was empty. I peered down at the red fellow's. Empty, too; a litter of crumpled blankets spilling out across the floor. I scrambled down from my bunk and hastily pulled on my trousers. Snatching up my jersey and boots, I dashed into the kitchen.

The red fellow was sprawled on the form, his back to the table, picking his teeth with a matchstick. There was no sign of Long John. 'What time is it?' I said, pulling my socks right side out.

'Near eight,' he said.

Long John stumped in out of the rain, an oilskin coat held loosely about his shoulders. He shrugged it off, dumping it against the wall. I had started to pull on my socks and he rounded on me at once. 'You should have been up long since, boy,' he said sharply.

'I slept in,' I said sheepishly.

He turned on the red fellow. 'I told you to waken the boy early, so we would be ready for a sharp start the minute Big Willie is here. What came over you?'

'Ach, I thought he was as well sleeping,' the red fellow said, yawning. He stretched lazily. 'What's your hurry? I doubt we will never manage out to fish the nets today.'

'You doubt, eh?' Long John said, and I did not like the silky turn to his voice.

'Aye, I more than doubt it,' the red fellow replied, and he spoke stoutly enough, I must give him that. If I had been in his shoes, I know I would have quailed before the look in Long John's eyes.

'So you more than doubt it, eh?' Long John snorted. 'Because there was a gale last night? Good life, the breeze this morning would barely ruffle your hair.'

As he spoke, a gust swirled around the bothy, sending the door creaking back on its hinges. It was more than a breeze, I thought.

'The wind is down, right enough,' the Harris man admitted. 'But did you take a look at the sea that is running?'

'Aye, I have seen it,' Long John said. 'A bit of a swell just. We will manage out easy enough.'

'Easy enough?' the red fellow laughed, and spat into the fire. 'Easy enough, you say, with Big Willie and myself just, and a green boy for third hand? You must be thinking we are off our heads, man.'

'You have forgotten me,' Long John said.

The red fellow took his time before he spoke, looking Long John coolly up and down, his eyes coming to rest on the crutch. 'Aye, I had forgotten you,' he said, and the way he said it was as bad as a slap in the face. 'But not even you can make the sea calm,' he added.

'We will manage out easy enough,' Long John repeated.

'Never the day,' the red fellow declared.

'I am telling you, we will,' Long John insisted, his face darkening.

The Harris man shrugged. 'We will see what Big Willie has to say,' he countered.

'I am the one who will do the saying around here,' Long John thundered. 'Never you mind what Big Willie has to say. Big Willie can get himself into the coble along wi' you and the boy, and he had better be quick about it.'

He stumped out into the rain, not even bothering to pick up his discarded oilskin. I gulped down a hasty breakfast and pulled on my oilskin and sou'wester just as Big Willie was crossing the bridge. I ran down to meet him, eager to hear the news of Ruairidh.

'No word,' he shouted, as he climbed down the ladder, the wind billowing out his streaming wet oilskin. 'Morag tried to get through last night, but the lines were down. The gale was bad on the mainland. It was just the tail end of her we got here.'

I tried to hide my disappointment. Big Willie gripped my shoulder and pointed out to the bay. The sea heaved in an angry swell, and the steep, green rollers broke on the shore in a surge of white spray, boiling madly with the force of the undertow.

Big Willie sniffed. 'A bad sea running,' he said. 'We will never make out today. Maybe they will have the lines repaired by now, so you can get back early with me and see if Morag has news.'

'Long John says we will manage out,' I said, thinking it wiser that he should hear the news from me, and work off his temper on it right away, rather than flare up in the face of Long John.

I might have saved my breath. He only snorted, and snapped: 'Away, boy. The man is having you on.'

Even then there would not have been such a terrible row, if only Long John had not been in such a bad mood. He knew what a cross man Big Willie was first thing in the morning, but he went at him like a bull at a gate.

Instead of cracking a joke with him, the way he usually did, and gradually working him into a good humour, he dragged out his big silver pocket watch and glared at it. 'First the boy and now you,' he barked at Willie. 'Are the pair o' you feeding on sleeping pills, or are you not able to tell the time?'

He was a slow man on the uptake, Big Willie. He just stared at him stupidly, not saying a word.

'You are late,' Long John snapped, 'and I was meaning to be off at eight o'clock sharp, in case the wind rises again.'

'Late!' Big Willie exclaimed, his red face getting even redder. 'Me, late? Good grief, man, you are lucky I am here at all. If I had been half wise, I would have stayed in my bed. We will never make out on a day like this.'

'I was after telling him that,' the red fellow chipped in.

Long John took no heed of him. He thrust out his face at Big Willie, and said: 'We will make out, right enough, or my name is not MacGregor.'

'We will, eh?' Big Willie said. 'Not so much of the "we". If the coble is for out, it will be yourself aboard her, not me.'

'You will be there, too,' Long John said, 'or you can march straight to the Factor, and tell him that it is you that is finished at the fishing.'

Big Willie's temper came up like a saucepan of milk on a roaring fire. His fists clenched, and I thought for a moment that he was going to strike Long John. But he thought better of it. It was the crutch that saved him, though, nothing else.

'Finished, is it?' Big Willie said between clenched teeth. 'Well, let me tell you, MacGregor, you will wait long enough before you see another man here in my place.'

He turned to go. Long John spat loudly. 'Fishermen!' he exclaimed. 'They call themselves fishermen! Good grief, they should be sitting round the fire holding wool for the old wives knitting.'

Big Willie whipped round, his face flaming. 'Are you

making out I am afraid?' he snarled. 'Do you take me for the boy there? If the rest o' you are for chancing it, I will take my place.'

'Don't be looking at Murdo,' Long John sneered. 'He has a face on him like a sick cow at the thought o' putting to sea.'

'Have it your own way,' the red fellow shrugged. 'But if the coble ends up on the rocks you are not the only one the crabs will be feasting on. The rest of us will be there along with you, mind.'

'Well, well, so you have a tongue on you after all, Murdo,' Long John mocked. 'And you can use it well enough, too, when you think your skin is in danger.'

'It is not myself I was thinking of,' the red fellow declared. 'It is the boy.' He looked at Big Willie. 'He has no right to force the boy out on a day like this.'

'Aye, it is not right risking the boy's neck,' Big Willie said.

'The boy can please himself,' Long John said. 'It's no place for a boy, anyway.'

He stumped off to the coble, with the other two hard on his heels. I stood on the river bank, watching the spray being flung high where the heavy swell pounded against the cliff. It was a bad day, right enough. I did not fancy the look of the sea at all.

I felt a hand on my shoulder, and I looked up into the long face of the red fellow. 'Well, boy, what do you think of the fishing now, eh?' he said, his lips drawn back from his stained teeth in what he took to be a smile. He tapped his forehead. 'Long John is a bit off up here ever since he lost his leg. He is mad enough to chance anything. And Big Willie is in such a rage he would make out in a dinghy, let alone a coble.' He glanced over his shoulder at the other two, standing by the coble, where it was drawn up outside the bothy. 'I have got to chance it, too, seeing that they are for going, but there is no sense in you risking your life. Clear off home, boy. You heard what Long John said. No one would blame you.' He squeezed my shoulder hard. 'Clear off home, boy, while you still have the chance.'

Chapter Eleven

To tell the truth I was sorely tempted. I had been born within sight and sound of the sea, and I had spent all my life on the rocky east coast of our island. In our township, the sea is never out of sight, and hardly ever out of mind. I knew enough about it to realize the risks they were taking.

If a heavy breaker caught the coble before she had fully cleared the river mouth, she would be dashed on the rocks and smashed to pieces within minutes. But that was only the first of the dangers they faced. To try to fish a bag net with such a swell running was to risk capsizing the coble, and if that did not happen there was always the danger of the engine stalling. If the engine failed, they could not hope to keep her off the rocks with the oars alone. And if all those perils were overcome, the greatest one of all had still to be surmounted – the river had to be regained without the coble being swept on to the rocks by the force of the breakers.

If it had been any other man than the red fellow, I might have heeded his advice. But I knew well enough that all he wanted was to see me away from the bothy, and I would have cut the nose off my face to spite him in that.

To be honest, though, I listened to him with only one ear. It was the words of Long John that burned in my mind, and rankled within me. *The boy can please himself* he had said, not even looking at me as he spoke, tossing the words out carelessly, as if I had been of no more concern to him than an old boot. It was his words, and his alone, that determined me on my course. *The boy can please himself*. Very well, I would please myself.

'If the rest of you are going out, my place is in the coble,' I said.

I think the red fellow could see by my face that it was useless arguing. So it was. At any rate, all he said was: 'You are a fool, boy. But before the coble is out of the river, you will be wishing you were on your way home.'

His forecast was more than half true. It makes me wild to have to admit, but a part of me had no stomach for the sea, and I could not get out of my mind the thought of our cosy kitchen at home, Lassie stretched out on the rug, and the peat fire glowing in the open range. No wonder. As I sat in the stern of the coble, watching the breakers come surging in, I did not see how she could come through them, and live.

As we neared the mouth of the river, Long John shouted: 'Oars, boys.' They were already fitting the long oars into the rowlocks before he opened his mouth, and they put their backs into it with a will. There is no need for orders when your life is depending on the speed with which you jump to it.

The coble rose high on the first roller, tossed up as lightly as a cork. She came down into the trough, the screw racing as it came clear of the water. A torrent of spray streamed over her curving bow, dashing against the bent backs of the oarsmen. It even reached Long John and me in the stern.

Up we went. Down again, timbers groaning. A flood of spray half swamped the rowers. They strained grimly on the oars, pulling with every ounce of their strength, arms shooting forward again like out-thrust pistons. Up again, and over the crest of the roller, the stern riding clear of the water. Then down, down, down, until I thought she would never lift her bows again.

I gripped the gunwale with frozen fingers, seeing a huge green wall of water bearing down on us. Slowly – so slowly that at first I thought she was not moving at all – every timber in her groaning like a live thing, her high prow lifted through it. A flood of water and spray poured over the port bow. The coble staggered, dipped into a trough again, and wallowed out of it.

We were hardly making way at all, the thrust of the

engine lost every time the screw lifted out of the water. I glanced astern, seeing the tide ebbing back from the rocks at the river mouth, and surging forward again to swamp them in a creamy wash of foam and spray. The half-covered rocks were no more than a cable's length away.

The rowers had seen them, too. Indeed, they never took their eyes off them. They redoubled their efforts, lips drawn back as they gulped air, straining on the oars like men possessed.

We took seven bad ones, one after the other, not a break between them. I counted them, and I am not likely to forget the number. The seventh roller was the worst of the lot, a monster just. I shut my eyes as the towering wall of water swept down on us.

I heard the coble groan from stem to stern, as she struggled to climb through it. I pitched forward, almost losing my grip, as the stern kicked up, suddenly riding free. Then it was down, down, down, and a crack like the shot of a cannon, as another wave broke against our bows. I opened my eyes, and ducked quickly, taking a shower of spray across my back.

Big Willie's sou'wester had slipped over his eyes. His mouth gaped open like the mouth of a stranded fish, and he grunted every time he pulled back on his oar. Short, savage grunts, as if he were fighting a battle with the heavy oar, and knew that it was going to be a losing one. Farther for'ard, on the starboard oar, the red fellow was in no better shape. His face had a mottled look, and his long frame seemed to sag every time he took his blade back for another pull.

But we had struggled clear of the river mouth, clear of the menacing rocks, and the steep, inshore rollers. The screw was biting deep, no longer riding clear of the water, and we gradually drew away from the shore.

Long John swung her slowly round to the north and the men shipped their oars. The coble ploughed through the swell, pitching steeply, but riding it well. Great showers of spray broke over her bows, and the bilge swirled about my ankles whenever she lifted on the swell.

Big Willie went for'ard, and joined the red fellow on his seat. They huddled together, backs bent against the lash of the spray, their heads close together. The noise of the labouring engine and the wind and sea smothered their voices, but I could guess what they were talking about by the angry looks they shot in the direction of Long John.

Their glares did not seem to disturb him. I doubt if he even noticed them. He was bareheaded, his black hair plastered wetly about his head, rain and spray trickling down his neck inside the collar of his yellow oilskin smock.

It did not seem to worry him. Indeed, he looked as if he was enjoying himself. He was like a beached boat on dry land, smart though he was with the crutch, not really coming to life until he was back in his element, and at grips with the sea.

He leaned over, his lips close to my ear. 'We will fish the Rock net first,' he shouted.

I nodded, my eyes on the red fellow and Big Willie. The Harris man had certainly found his tongue now. He was talking away good style, bringing his fist down on the big fellow's knee to ram some point home. Big Willie nodded, and from the looks he was giving Long John it was clear who was figuring in the talk.

The coble plunged steeply, shipping a bad one over the bow. 'Getting sick?' Long John yelled.

I shook my head. 'Wait you,' he roared. 'When she is not making way, that is the time you will feel it, boy.'

I ducked as a cloud of spray crashed high over the bows, and showered us in the stern. Long John took it full in the face and never even blinked. In fact, he grinned. I believe he would not have exchanged his wet seat in the stern for the ease of a cushioned throne.

We were the best part of two hours battling against the wind and sea to the Rock net. As we drew near, I could see the tremendous wash of tide and swell around the dark reef. The sea surged forward, flooding over the jutting point of the reef, breaking around the rocks in a fury of crashing waves and drenching them in torrents of spray. The undertow swirled back, the water boiling, baring the black spine of the reef until another breaker swept down on it.

The black rocks were bare. The seabirds had fled inland. Not even a gull could have survived on the rocks with the angry wash of the sea breaking all around. I did not fancy the look of them at all. The sooner the net was fished and we were away, the better, I thought.

It seemed that Long John had taken the bag net too wide, and we were going to miss it by yards. But as he cut the engine, the swell plucked the coble round and flung her against the net. Big Willie's clutching hands seized the rope on the head pole, and the red fellow hung on grimly to a side rope. Long John was out of the stern seat and in between the two of them like a flash, pulling in the head-pole and freeing the padlock.

He was as much a part of the pitching, rolling coble as the timber that went into the making of her. With his good knee wedged against the gunwale, hands working at the head pole ropes, he kept his balance as easily as I could have done with two good legs planted firmly on dry ground.

With the three of them hanging over the port gunwale, clinging to the ropes of the bag net, the coble was at the mercy of the swell. She was flung up and down like a tossing cork. One moment I was gazing up at a wall of water, certain that it could not fail to swamp the heeling boat, and the next moment I was looking down into a deep trough. Then down again, shipping water freely, Long John's salmon club floating in the bilge around my feet.

Now that the coble had stopped making way, and was rolling wildly, like a drifting log, my stomach started to turn queasy. Gripping a seat, I slid across to the gunwale, alongside the red fellow. I wedged my knees against the gunwale, and helped to haul in the net, hoping that the work would take my mind off my stomach. Anything was better than sitting idly in the stern, getting sick.

We rose up on the swell, and the coble took a steep plunge. The red fellow was thrown off balance, and he crashed against me. I pitched forward, arms and shoulders under water. If I had been wearing a smock like the rest of them, I would have been over the side there and then, but Long John managed to get a hand to the belt of my oilskin coat. He dragged me back aboard.

'Get in the stern,' he shouted. 'You are more use there. Cover the engine.'

I fought my way back against the steep list of the boat, and covered the engine as best I could with the skirt of my oilskin. Long John had the fish door open. As the coble went down in a trough, they heaved up the net. Three salmon plunged into the coble, all of them young grilse, seven pounders, at the very outside. I groped for the club and handed it to Long John. Three quick thumps, and the threshing fish were still.

Long John fastened the fish door and they released the net. But it was no easy task sinking the head pole with the coble rolling and plunging so wildly. It took the combined weight of the three of them to force it down, and it was a wonder to me that the coble did not capsize in the doing of it. Long John secured the padlock and ropes. He let go, and the head pole bobbed upright.

I had the starter cord wound ready, and I gave it a sharp tug. The noise of the engine firing was sweeter in my ears than the music of a massed pipe band. I opened the throttle as Long John dropped into the stern seat beside me. He took over the helm without a word.

As his hand closed over the rubber grip, we caught a bad one, almost full abeam. The sea smashed over the stern, half drowning me, and the coble shuddered from stem to stern. The engine faltered and coughed, and slowly picked up again. Another sea broke over the stern. The engine spluttered, and died.

The silence struck me worse than a thunderclap, but it galvanized the others into action. Long John fumbled at the starter cord. The other two scrambled for the oars. A wave caught the coble, whipped her round broadside on to the swell, and swept her back towards the reef. It seemed to my fear-stricken eyes that she had never moved so fast before. We were being carried closer to the jagged black spine of the reef with every second that passed.

Long John yanked the starter cord. The engine coughed and died. Big Willie was pulling on his oar like a madman, and the curving beak of the prow faced the swell again. The red fellow cried: 'Hold her at that,' and the two of them bent their backs to the oars and pulled as they had never pulled before.

Long John tried to start the engine a second time, and failed. He glanced at the looming reef as he wound the cord for a third attempt. For all the efforts of the oarsmen, we were barely holding our own. Once they started to tire, we were finished. The jagged rocks of the reef would tear the bottom out of the cable, and the sea would pound her to matchwood.

I held my breath as he pulled the starter cord for the third time. The engine gave a faint cough, drowned in a loud curse from Long John. He fished under his smock, and thrust a dry rag into my hands. Working feverishly, he removed the magneto cap and took out the sparking plug. He snatched the rag out of my hands and unrolled it. There was a fresh plug inside. He fitted the plug and connected the lead, drying it carefully with the rag. He wiped his hands on the rag and replaced the cap. I wanted to close my eyes and shut my ears as he wound the starter cord.

The engine fired at the first pull, and the cable, with the thrust of the screw added to the pull of the oars, drew away from the reef. Soon we were running easily before the wind and sea, and the long oars had been shipped once more. I had learned one lesson, at any rate. Never again would I despise an oar; no, not for all the outboards in creation.

Big Willie and the red fellow were huddled together again. They were facing the prow now, and all I could see of them was their bent backs. They were so close together you could have got the one sou'wester over the two heads, supposing you could have found one big enough.

Big Willie got up and made his way aft. He steadied himself with a hand on my shoulder and bent over Long

John. 'You can make straight for the river,' he declared, 'whether you like it or not. Murdo and me are done with fishing for the day, even supposing the rest o' the nets are thick wi' salmon. We have had enough, MacGregor. Aye, more than enough.'

Long John nodded. 'As you wish,' he said mildly, and I wondered if he was already regretting the rash words he had spoken before we set out.

Willie made his way for'ard to his seat, and he and the red fellow soon had their heads together again. Long John did not seem to be in a mood for talking, and neither was I, for that matter. I was thinking how the red fellow had been thrown against me when we were fishing the net, and how only the quick action of Long John had saved me from going over the side. Had he genuinely lost his balance, or did he deliberately blunder into me? He was the only man who could answer that question, so I would never know. Accident or no, it was as well to remember what had happened to Ruairidh, and I resolved to keep well clear of him in future.

We made good time back to the river mouth, but the tide was on the ebb now. It had uncovered the rocks at the narrow entrance to the river, and the channel lay dangerously close to them. To make matters worse, the wind had freshened. It was licking white tops on the crests of the rollers.

As he took the coble in, Long John shouted to Big Willie to have an oar ready. I believe Willie thought he would give him a fright, and not pull until the last moment. At any rate, he was slow in dipping his oar, when two good pulls would have been enough to straighten the coble. As it was, she was caught by a steep roller and swept off course before Willie's oar was in the water. He saw the danger too late, and jabbed his oar out like a spear, trying to fend the boat off the rocks. The blade snapped like a matchstick, and he fell against the gunwale, crushing his fingers between the stump of the oar and the rowlock.

The coble plunged down on the rocks, changed course slightly, whether by the pull of the tide or Long John's work at the helm I shall never know, and scraped past them into the calm water of the river. A deep groove, the length of my arm, had been gouged in her timbers, and Big Willie's crushed fingers were spouting blood, but that was all the damage we suffered.

Nobody spoke as we moved upstream and nosed into the berth below the bothy. Big Willie muttered something to the red fellow, as they leapt ashore and made for the rollers, but not a word was spoken as we hauled the coble up the slip on the hand winch.

We all stripped off our soaking oilskins in the store shed, and trooped silently to the bothy. Long John sat down on the big cork float at the end of the table. Big Willie and the red fellow stood in the doorway. I was behind them. The silence was the sort that you feel deep in the stomach – the brooding silence of a gathering storm. I waited tensely for it to break.

Long John was playing with his ebony-hafted knife, digging the point into the table.

'Well?' he said.

I saw the red fellow's elbow busily working at Big Willie's ribs. He would always be the one, I thought, to stand in the shadows, and urge another to fire the shot. Willie took a step forward, wrapping a dirty handkerchief around his bleeding fingers.

'You were keen on making out, MacGregor,' he said. 'And what have we to show for it? Three grilse – poor ones at that – and a broken oar – and this!' He held up his clenched fist, the dirty handkerchief already a bright crimson with seeping blood. 'A fine fishing, eh?' he sneered.

'Aye, and very near drowned, the lot of us,' the red fellow chipped in over his shoulder. 'If she had gone on the reef we were finished.

Long John dug the knife savagely into the table. It stuck there, quivering. 'Well?' he said again.

'You told me I could march to the Factor and tell him I was finished, if I did not make out with you,' Big Willie went on. 'Well, I made out with you, so you can make no lies about me being afraid. But I am marching off now, MacGregor, and Murdo along wi' me, and we are not marching back in a hurry. I wish you luck at the fishing. You will be needing it.'

He swung round, nearly knocking me off my feet, in his blind rage to be gone from the bothy. The red fellow turned after him. He whipped back like a scavenging dog loth to leave his pickings, and snarled: 'Seeing you are so keen on drowning, MacGregor, you can drown alone.'

There was a long silence.

'Well, boy?' Long John said.

The red fellow was back at my side. 'What are you waiting for, boy?' he said. 'Big Willie is across the bridge.'

I took a step forward. 'Come on,' he said, catching me by the shoulder.

I tried to shake myself free, but he tightened his grip. I stumbled back against the door. It slammed shut behind us.

'Take your hands off the boy, Murdo,' Long John said quietly.

He got a better grip on me and gave me a shake. 'Wake up, boy,' he said, 'and let us away. That old cratur is finished. Let him be.'

I saw Long John's fingers close over the ebony haft of the knife, and jerk it out of the table. His arm drew back, and the next thing I knew the knife had thudded into the door. I swear it was not an inch from the red fellow's ear.

'I told you to take your hands off the boy, Murdo,' Long John said.

I looked at the red fellow. His bulging eyes were fixed on the quivering knife. There were beads of sweat as big as winkles coming off him. He swallowed, and made to say something, but the words were not there. He seemed to have a job to find the handle, but he got the door open and stumbled out.

I shut it again and looked wonderingly at the knife. The blade was deep in the wood. It was some throw.

'Well, boy?' Long John said.

Chapter Twelve

I reached up and tugged at the knife. The blade was so deep in the wood I had to work it up and down before I could pull it out. I laid it on the table in front of him and sat down on the wooden form.

'That was some throw,' I said. 'Good life, you might have killed him.'

I doubt if he heard me. He had picked up the knife and was working moodily at the table with it, nicking the deal top with the sharp point. I watched the point being jabbed more fiercely into the wood. He was building himself up into a towering rage. I waited for the explosion to come, expecting him to rant against Big Willie and the red fellow for their desertion. To my surprise, he did not reproach them. Indeed, his anger seemed to be directed at me.

'Well, what are you sitting there for?' he burst out. 'Why do you not make after them?'

I kept my mouth shut. There was an awkward silence, the sort of silence that makes talk more difficult the longer it lasts.

'If you go now, you will catch them before they reach the road,' he said, not looking at me.

'There is only room for two on Big Willie's bike,' I said, not moving.

He jabbed the knife savagely into the table. He was not carving initials on it, but it would soon be in a worse state than my old desk at school.

'Well, you heard what Murdo had to say, didn't you?' he demanded. 'He made out I was old and done. He said I near drowned the lot o' you.'

'Aye, I heard him,' I said.

'Well, what use is an old man at the fishing – with only a boy for his crew?'

'Ach, we will manage,' I said. 'You are not done. That is all talk.'

'It is more than talk,' he insisted. 'Big Willie and Murdo are away. If I were a right man still, with all my strength, the two o' them would have thought twice before they turned their backs on me.' He stabbed the knife into the table. 'Twice, did I say? No, three times! Aye, they would have thought three times and more, before they turned their backs on me, fearing the blow I would strike them. But not now. And I sit here, like an old wife at the fire, and watch them go.' He gazed at me for the first time, coldly, as if we had only newly met, and he did not much fancy the look of me. 'It is as well for you to be gone with them,' he said.

'It is all the Harris man's doing,' I said hotly. 'Big Willie may be a bit thick in the head, but he will see sense yet. He was wild at you this morning, and the red fellow is after spoiling him. I believe he was keeping him going all day just. Willie is like that. A bad word or two will keep him on the boil, but he has a good enough heart on him for all that. The same man would never have cleared off if the red fellow had left him alone. But he will cool down through time.'

Long John ran his thumb along the blade of the knife. 'You think the red fellow talked him into it?' he asked.

'I am sure of it,' I said eagerly. 'I believe he put Willie up to it when we were out in the coble. Even then, he had to be pushed before he started laying off his chest. Good life, the Harris man's elbow was near making a hole in the big fellow's side before he blew up and said he was clearing off.'

He looked at me keenly. 'You are not slow, boy,' he said at length. 'I believe you have the bold Murdo well weighed up.' He tossed the knife aside. 'Ach, well, if you are bent on staying, I suppose you would be the better of a bite o' food under your belt.'

He smiled as he spoke, and I was relieved to see the change that came over him. He had been out of humour all day, snapping at me because I was late up, rounding fiercely on the red fellow when he had suggested that the sea was too wild for fishing and giving Big Willie an awful dressing-down for not being on time. Once we were out in the coble, he had calmed down and he had remained calm, oddly enough, even after Big Willie had laid into him. It was only when I had elected to stay that he had flared up again, and that had puzzled me, because I had expected him to be pleased that there was one member of his crew who was not prepared to walk out on him.

I supposed it was my age that had angered him, the fact that he was to be left with only a boy to command. But it had not lasted for long, and he seemed to toss his ill-humour aside with the knife. In less time than it takes to blink, he was bustling around getting a meal ready, and whistling away as if he had not a care in the world.

When we had taken our dinner, he got his pipe going and started talking. To hear him you would never have thought that two of his men had newly deserted. He never mentioned them at all, not like most men, who would have kept on for long enough, picking them to pieces and making them out as black as the pot.

But not Long John. He had great yarns about the years he spent aboard a whaler in the Southern Ocean, and you would never believe some of the things that happened to him, like the time the cook got drunk and tossed the vegetables into the swill bin, and the peelings into the stew. We had some laughs together, I am telling you.

The only time a shadow crossed his face was when I asked him why he had stopped going to the whaling seeing the pay was so good and he liked the life. He said it was at South Georgia that he had lost his leg in an accident, and that had finished him for the whaling.

He was silent for a while after that, scraping out his pipe and taking his time filling it again. I wished I had kept my big mouth shut. When his pipe was drawing well, he said : 'There is not much in the way o' work for a sea-faring man, when he has only the one leg.'

'No one would know you had only the one, to see you working,' I said quickly.

He plucked at the empty flap of his trouser leg where it was pinned back under his stump. 'They have eyes,' he said, 'and they are not slow in using them, when it is work you are after.'

'Well, you are skipper at the salmon fishing,' I said.

'Aye, skipper at the salmon fishing,' he agreed, and there was no mirth in his smile. 'Four months in the year just. A fine job, skipper at the salmon fishing, for a man with a mate's ticket – deep-sea at that – in his pocket. A crew of two men and a boy, and the command of a coble. Oh, a fine job, boy. Give me a new leg and I would show you what I think of it.'

He lapsed into silence, his dark eyes staring blankly into space. I wondered if he was seeing the great wastes of the Southern Ocean in his mind's eye, and hearing again the lookout's cry, as the blue whale was sighted in the cold seas south of Cape Horn.

He blinked, and his eyes came back into focus. 'Ach, I am too old for the whaling,' he said, 'supposing a derrick had never fallen on my leg at South Georgia.' He laughed, his face breaking into a wide grin. 'The salmon fishing is more in my line these days.'

It seemed that nothing could hold his spirits down for long now that he had thrown off the black mood of the morning. He was soon yarning again, telling me of the time he had set out with his own boat, shark fishing in the waters around the Western Isles.

He had found bits of an old harpoon gun in a scrapyard in Glasgow, and built it up himself. He rigged the gun on the foredeck of his boat, anchoring it on a metal plate that he bolted to the deck. The first time he tried her, he put in too big a charge, and the kick from the gun knocked him clean off the deck and into the sea. 'By golly, I was careful with the powder after that,' he said, laughing.

'Why did you not keep on at it?' I asked, thinking that shark fishing was a job I would fancy myself.

'Ach, the price we were getting for the oil went away to nothing,' he said. 'There was no money in it, boy, what with a heavy freight to pay on the barrels, and the Norwegians were making an awful killing. They had the gear, see. All I had was my old boat, and a queer, ramshackle of a home-made harpoon gun.'

'It must have been good at the shark fishing,' I said eagerly.

'Aye, it was good, right enough,' he said simply.

'I wish I had been along with you at it,' I said.

'Ach, you were just a lad at school when I was at the shark fishing,' he said, smiling, 'and it was not for me to know you were hankering for a crack at it, or maybe I would have called in and taken you for a trip. Many a time I sailed up the Minch when you must have been taking your lessons in the school.'

He punched me lightly on the shoulder, the way Ruairidh sometimes did when he was pleased with me. 'Don't look so down in the mouth, boy,' he said. 'One day you may be out in the Minch with your own boat. Who knows? Aye, and shark hunting, too. You will think of me then – me and my old gun, the one that very near blew me into kingdom come.'

He laughed so whole-heartedly that I had to join in, although I felt I had been cheated by a trick of time and that is the worst trick of all, for there is no going back on it.

For all the terrible start, the angry quarrelling and the near disaster in the coble, I think I enjoyed that day at the bothy better than any other. With the red fellow out of the way, I could talk freely, and Long John was an easy man to talk to.

The rain had stopped and the strong breeze soon cleared the sky of clouds. The sun came out and we went up to the drying green, and lowered the hanging net and stacked it. We hoisted another one on the halyards, and I realized then, for the first time, the full weight of a net when there were only the two of us at the hauling of it.

There was a rip in the side of the bag, so Long John gave me a lesson in mending. I tried my best, but I was not much of a hand with the needle, and I was glad that Morag could not see me. Some of the ropes were worn, and Long John sent me to the store shed to fetch a coil of tarry spunyarn. The spunyarn was used to prevent the ropes fraying on the rocks, and he showed me how to bind them with it.

In the early evening the wind dropped, and it was hotter than it had been all day. We had taken tea and Long John was sitting in the deep sill of the window outside the bothy. I had my arms crossed on the high prow of the coble, and I was looking up the gorge to the bridge.

'I believe you are still brooding about Ruairidh and the red fellow,' Long John said quietly. 'You are an awful boy for getting your teeth into something and hanging on, eh?'

I was of half a mind to blurt out the whole story to him there and then, but he was such an open sort of man I was afraid he would tackle the Harris man with it to his face, so I said cautiously: 'Maybe I am. But I was right enough. He did push Ruairidh into the river.'

Long John took his pipe out of his mouth and stared at me. 'Not from the bridge,' I said hastily. 'See!' And I pointed to the track above the narrow ledge of rock. 'You thought Ruairidh had fallen from the bridge,' I went on, 'but if the red fellow pushed him in from the track there he would have hit the rocks below the bridge just the same. And you would never have spotted him if he flattened down the moment Ruairidh fell.'

'No, maybe not,' he admitted doubtfully.

'I was asking Big Willie where the red fellow was when he came out of the bothy,' I rushed on. 'It took him a while, but he remembered seeing him come down from the direction of the bridge.'

'But surely I would have seen him crossing the bridge?' Long John said.

'No, not when you had dived in the river,' I said. 'Once you were striking out for Ruairidh, it was safe enough for him to cross the bridge and get back to this side. Once you were in the river you would have your eyes fixed on Ruairidh.'

He nodded slowly. 'But what about Big Willie? Willie

was bound to see him on the bridge.'

'No, Willie was in his bunk when you let out a yell,' I reminded him. 'By the time Willie had pulled on his boots, and got to the door of the bothy, the red fellow would be across the bridge. Willie is a slow mover – you know that.'

'Aye, Willie is slow,' he admitted. He looked at me keenly. 'But what makes you so sure it was not an accident? Good life, if Murdo really pushed Ruairidh into the river, he must have meant to kill him. And if Ruairidh should . . .' He stopped, clamping his mouth shut before the word 'die' could come out. He started again. 'Murdo could have killed him. That would have been murder, boy. The two of them had no fancy for each other, I could see that, but why should Murdo want to murder Ruairidh? I can't see it, unless you are keeping something back.'

'Well, there was something queer going on,' I said.

'Something queer?'

'Aye.' I hesitated. 'Ruairidh had written things down in his diary. I believe the red fellow was after it.'

Long John looked puzzled, and no wonder. 'What things?' he said.

'Numbers and things.'

'Are you making this up?' he said suspiciously.

'Not at all,' I said indignantly, and I told him about the numbers in the diary, and the word 'Morgana'.

'Morgana?' he said, rubbing at his chin. 'Morgana?' He scratched his head, and there was still a suspicious look on his face when he said: 'What do you suppose that means?'

'Maybe it is the name of a ship,' I suggested.

'Maybe,' he said, but he did not sound very impressed. 'A fancy name for a ship, boy. I never heard the like of it before.'

'No, nor me,' I agreed, not wanting to let on that I believed it to be the name of the wrecked Spanish galleon in Tobermory Bay. Leaning against the coble in the bright evening sunlight, talking to Long John outside the bothy, such things as murder and a Spanish treasure ship seemed to belong to the world of story books.

'Whereabouts in the diary were these numbers?' he asked.

I told him that the first entry was near the end of May, and the last one had been made the day before Ruairidh met with his accident.

'Was there a different number for each day of the week?' he said, after he had thought for a while.

I nodded. 'Aye, but there were two of them the same, I think.'

Long John nodded absently, tapping the stem of his pipe against his teeth. I had certainly captured his attention now. He was so interested that he had let his pipe go out, and he did not bother to relight it.

'Can you mind any of the numbers?' he said suddenly.

I thought hard. 'Only two of them,' I said. 'The two that were the same. Eighty-one was the number, that is how I remember it.'

He took the tattered notebook out of his pocket that he used to keep a tally of the fish landed, and started to thumb through it. 'Can you mind the dates as well as the numbers?' he asked.

I could not see what he was getting at, but I did my best. 'I can mind the days, but not the dates,' I said. 'The first eighty-one was entered on a Thursday, and the second one was on a Tuesday, if I mind right. But the dates are nothing to do with it. There was not much space for writing in the diary, and the numbers were printed in big figures.'

Long John was thumbing through the notebook, not heeding me, but I plunged on. 'It was just the way they were set out,' I explained, 'different numbers in the space for each day in the diary. The dates have nothing to do with it. I believe the numbers made up a – well, some sort of a code.'

Long John looked up from the tattered notebook. I doubt if he had heard a single word. 'You have a good memory, boy,' he said calmly.

I stared at him in astonishment. 'Eighty-one on Thursday, June 3rd,' he said, seemingly reading from the notebook, 'and eighty-one on Tuesday, June 15th. I thought as much.' He shut the notebook and stuffed it into his pocket.

I goggled at him, my mouth hanging open.

'You know what Ruairidh was doing?' he said, not waiting for an answer, but going straight on: 'He was keeping a tally of the salmon we landed.'

'A tally of the salmon?' I repeated stupidly.

Long John nodded. 'And you were after thinking it was some sort of a code,' he said, smiling.

'Well, I . . . I . . .' I spluttered, finally bursting out with: 'But why should Ruairidh keep a tally?'

'Oh, not only Ruairidh is at that game,' he said quickly. 'I believe they all do it. Well, maybe not Big Willie, but Murdo, for sure. I bet he has not missed a single fish since the day we started. If I were to tell him that Ruairidh had been keeping a tally, he might admit that he was keeping one, too.'

'Good life!' I cried in alarm. 'You are not thinking of speaking to him about the diary?'

He shook his head impatiently. 'Let me speak, boy, for goodness' sake. You were asking why Ruairidh kept a tally. I will tell you for why. At the end of the season we get a bonus. The size of the bonus depends on the number of fish we have landed. Well, the boys like to make sure that they are not being cheated, so they keep a tally themselves. That way they can be sure they are being paid on the right number of fish. If you bring Ruairidh's diary down with you, we can go through it together. You will find that the numbers he has down are the same as the ones in my book.'

'Well, well!' was all I could bring myself to say.

Long John chuckled. 'You make home for the diary one night, and bring it back with you. You can see for yourself then.'

'Aye, I will do that,' I said dully, my thoughts in a turmoil. I felt I had blundered enough already without telling him of the loss of the part of the diary that mattered, and my tussle with the bald-headed stranger. At the thought of the stranger, I did not feel so bad about my mistake over the numbers in the diary. There was still a mystery about it after all. The missing pages must have been of value to him, when he had risked entering our house to steal them. I remembered the shock he had got when I had spoken of 'Morgana'. The mystery of 'Morgana' remained as much a mystery as ever. And was it possible that I had overlooked some other vital entry?

'A pity you did not tell me about the diary before now,' Long John was saying. 'I would soon have put you right on it, once I had cottoned on to the numbers.'

'I never thought,' I said awkwardly, feeling guilty at the things I had concealed from him, and was still concealing. But if he knew the whole story I would not put it past him to confront the red fellow with it outright, and there was no sense in that until we knew more.

'I wish you could put me right on "Morgana",' I said ruefully. Long John was silent, frowning, and I said: 'You mind me asking the red fellow about the job he was on with Ruairidh – the one in Tobermory Bay? It was the wreck of a Spanish galleon they were after there. Do you suppose "Morgana" could be anything to do with that?'

I was afraid that he might laugh at me, but he took it seriously enough. 'It might,' he said thoughtfully. 'Aye, it might well be.' He had got his pipe going again, and he pulled on it strongly for several minutes without speaking. 'You are sure about this "Morgana"?' he said at length. 'You are not just making it up, because you were wrong about the numbers in the diary?'

'Never the day!' I exclaimed hotly. 'It was written down four times – on four Sundays. The last time was the day before Ruairidh was – the day before he had the accident.'

'And he and the red fellow were together in Tobermory Bay, eh?'

'Aye. He admitted it. You heard him.'

He nodded. 'I heard him, right enough, and I mind fine the hunt for the galleon. She was supposed to be the treasure ship of the Armada.'

'And you think "Morgana" is her name?' I said eagerly. I thought he was going to say yes, but he stopped suddenly, as if afraid of building up my hopes too high. He chewed on the stem of his pipe and sighed, 'I hardly know what to think, and that is the truth of it,' he said heavily. 'But one thing is sure, we will need to keep an eye on the red fellow. And you will need to watch your tongue, boy, in case he gets wind of what we are about.'

I said I would take care.

'Well, see you do,' he warned. 'You have been working at this thing too long on your own. If you are right about the red fellow, and he finds out that you suspect him, do you think he will not try to silence you?'

'But what if we have seen the last of him?' I said. 'What if he got Big Willie talked into walking out just as a cover, so that he could get away?'

He tapped out his pipe and stuffed it in his pocket. 'Enough of the questions,' he declared, and he put me in mind once more of Ruairidh who was for ever complaining about me and my questions. 'You have me dizzy with them.'

'But what if he has made his escape?' I persisted.

Long John seized his crutch and got to his feet. He was a fine-looking man, if it had not been for the missing leg; broad in the shoulder, and lean in the hip. There was strength in every line of him. He put a hand on my shoulder. 'If the bold Murdo is not here first thing in the morning,' he said grimly, 'it is you and me for the police, boy.'

Chapter Thirteen

It was all very well for Long John to talk confidently about going to the police, but what could we tell them? If we informed them that the Harris man had tried to kill Ruairidh by pushing him off the track and into the river, they would want to know who had seen him do it. It was no use going to the police without proof.

I said as much to him.

'Aye, you are right enough,' Long John said heavily. 'There is only one man who can prove we are not making lies, and he is not able, poor fellow.'

'Ruairidh?'

He nodded. 'Aye, Ruairidh. And even if he recovers, there is no knowing that he will be able to tell his story.'

Ruairidh *had* to recover. I would not let myself think otherwise. But I could not keep back a feeling of gloom. 'How do you mean?' I said dully.

'Well, he got a bad knock on the head, mind,' Long John said, 'and very often the memory is away after a crack the like o' the one poor Ruairidh got. Maybe he will have no word of how he came to be in the river.'

'Well, then, what is the use of going to the police?' I demanded, my spirits even more cast down.

'I only said we would tackle the police if the red fellow is not here in the morning,' he said patiently. 'But I believe he will be back right enough. Use the head, boy. It would look bad if he suddenly cleared off. Why should he? As far as he knows, everyone thinks that Ruairidh's fall was an accident.'

I nodded.

'Oh, he will be back, never fear,' Long John went on. 'The same fellow is too fond of the pennies to risk losing his bonus at the end of the season. He was wild this morning, though, seeing I made them try to fish the nets. That is why he talked Big Willie into walking out, and cleared off along with him. He would be thinking that would put me in my place. But he will be back tomorrow, you see. It is Saturday, and the *Kingfisher* is due to collect the catch, and he knows well enough it would be the sack right off if he is missing.'

Saturday, tomorrow! And I had arranged to meet Morag at the top of the gorge on Friday night – tonight! I had lost all track of days since starting at the salmon fishing, and I believe I would have had no mind of Morag if Long John had not spoken.

She was not to be seen as I came out on the cliff top. I wondered if she had grown tired of waiting and returned home in a huff. I hoped not. There would be an awful racket if ever my mother got the idea that I would not budge from the bothy to meet her.

I walked over to the edge of the cliff and stood looking down on the clump of bushes that marked the limit of the overhang. It was from the shelter of these bushes that the red fellow's partner had spied on the coble.

From the top down to the bushes, the cliff face was shaped like the bottom half of a saucer, a deep saucer that had been stood on end, not quite upright. The bushes grew out from the rim of the saucer, bent back like a letter C by the force of the winter gales. Below them the cliff sloped sharply inwards in a straight fall to the sea.

I looked around. Morag was not to be seen. Without a second thought I lowered myself over the edge of the cliff and started to climb down to the bushes. It was safe enough really, for there was a good cover of grass, and only the first fifty feet or so were at all steep. But I took it slowly, never looking down, for I have no great head for heights. Taking one step at a time and not moving my feet until I had a secure hand hold, I climbed down cautiously.

When I felt the branches of the bushes against my back, I took my first look down. Through the leaves the shimmering sea moved gently far below, the heavy swell of the morning down to a slight rise and fall. The cork floats of a leader net arched out from the shore as straight as an arrow. Half-way along the net, I saw a salmon leap. With any luck he would soon be in the bag.

I moved down until I had got my boots firmly wedged against the main branches of one of the bushes. Turning round cautiously, I squatted down, wedged between the cliff face and the bushes, completely hidden from below by the spreading foliage.

I was looking out across the Sound, the sea directly below me. I could see the river where it entered the sea, and the south end of the bay. Any boat entering or leaving the river could not fail to come into my view. It was clear that the stranger could not have picked a better vantage spot for spying on the coble. A watcher behind the bushes could never be seen from below unless he was using glasses, and the sun happened to catch them.

I straightened up carefully, and started the climb back. I was within a few yards of the top before I looked up, and I got some shock, I am telling you. There was a face hanging over the edge of the cliff, peering down at me.

It was Catriona. We gazed at each other. Only her head and shoulders were visible, and her fair plaits tied with scarlet ribbon. Her eyes were wide. I daresay she never thought I would have the nerve to tackle such a climb.

'Good life, you must fancy yourself at the mountaineering,' she said.

I scrambled up to the top, and sat on the edge of the cliff trying to hide my annoyance at her words. 'Where is Morag?' I said.

Catriona giggled. It was not often that she giggled, but there was a good reason for it. 'Your Aunt Phemie came this morning,' she said. 'Poor Morag had to go with her to the prayer meeting tonight.'

'That will sort her,' I said, thanking my lucky stars that I was staying at the bothy. Aunt Phemie had been a lady missionary in Africa, and to hear her speak you would think our township was far wilder than any place in the jungle. And she took such a time saying grace that I never knew what it was to have a hot breakfast when she was staying with us.

'How long is she staying?' I asked.

'I don't know,' Catriona said. 'She had heard about Ruairidh, and came to see your mother.'

'The same fellow would not thank her for it,' I said, regretting the words the moment I had spoken, even if they were true, for she meant no harm, poor soul.

'Well, the news of him is a bit better. They said at the hospital he is not quite so poorly now.'

'Has he come round?' I said eagerly.

'No, he is still unconscious, but they say he is not quite so poorly.'

'How can that be, if he is still unconscious?' I said scornfully. 'That is nonsense just.'

'No, it is not nonsense,' Catriona retorted. 'His pulse rate may be stronger, and – well, there are all sorts of ways they can find out how he is. Good life, he has not to be sitting up in bed and singing before they know he is getting better.'

'I would rather he were conscious,' I said glumly.

'Aye, but it is an improvement. You should be glad.'

'I am glad.'

'You don't look it.'

'Well, I am.'

There was a silence. I plucked a short blade of grass and chewed at it.

'How are you getting on at the fishing?' Catriona asked.

'All right.'

'And you don't mind staying at the bothy?'

'No.'

'Do you sleep all right?'

'Fine.'

'Who does the cooking?'

'Long John, mostly.'

'The fellow with the one leg?'

'Aye.'

'Well, well. How does he manage, I wonder?'

'He was at the whaling in the Antarctic,' I said, 'and shark fishing in the Minch. He made his own harpoon gun. Long John would tackle anything.'

'Is he a good hand at the cooking?'

'Aye. And he is faster with a needle than any woman I ever saw.'

'Away!'

'A mending needle, I mean – repairing the nets.'

Catriona laughed. 'He will not be so handy with a sewing needle.'

'Don't be so sure, lassie. He would tackle anything, the same fellow.'

'Good enough,' Catriona said. 'Maybe he will have you working with the needle at your socks before you are done. Morag would like that fine.'

'You can tell her he has me darning socks, if that will please her,' I said. 'Good life, I am not the one to grudge her a laugh, seeing she is landed with Aunt Phemie.'

Catriona laughed again. 'It is a shame just. Poor Morag. It is not fair to be laughing at her.'

'I am not laughing,' I said. 'I am sorry for the girl. Did you see Big Willie today?'

'Aye. I saw him in the shop.'

'Was there anyone along with him?'

She nodded. 'A stranger. Annie in the shop said he was working at the salmon fishing.'

'Aye, so he is. Murdo, the Harris man.'

'You have an awful scowl on you. Don't you like him?'

I shook my head.

'Why is that?'

'Ach, I just don't fancy him,' I said.

'Is it because he is the one who is doing the smuggling?' she said eagerly.

I very near swallowed the piece of grass I was chewing. I stared at her. 'What has Morag been telling you?' I demanded.

'Nothing much,' she said, making a play of tightening her hair ribbons.

'What?'

'Well, she just said Ruairidh's accident was not an accident at all, and she said a man came to the house and made out he was from the Insurance, and stole things out of Ruairidh's diary, and she said there was smuggling going on at the bothy, and she thought the Harris man was the one who was at the smuggling.' She took a quick breath. 'Is that why you wanted to know about "Morgana"?'

'Good life, I never knew the equal o' that girl for spinning yarns,' I said hotly.

'Well, it is right enough, isn't it?'

'Look, Catriona,' I said patiently. 'All I told Morag was that there was something queer going on. I said it might be smuggling, right enough. Might, mind you. I don't know!'

'Oh, it is smuggling, right enough,' she declared.

'Oh, it is smuggling, right enough,' I mimicked angrily.

'Well, well, I can see you giving up the nursing any day now, and joining the police. Mind you, I never heard of girl detectives.'

She rounded on me furiously, her eyes blazing. 'I know well enough it is smuggling that is going on,' she cried. 'Ruairidh was on the look-out for them. That is why he had the fight with Lachie.'

I stared at her, speechless. The longer I stared the angrier she became, but I was past caring. To hear Catriona, who was always so quiet and level-headed, speaking like this was enough to make a man go and jump off the cliff. It must be Morag's work, I decided. Without me at home to check her, she would be pumping all sorts of nonsense into Catriona's head.

Catriona was getting steadily redder. 'I am telling you, that is why Ruairidh had the fight with Lachie,' she burst out again. 'He was on the look-out for the smugglers.'

Lachie was Catriona's brother, and a good friend of Ruairidh. He was the last man Ruairidh would ever fight without cause. I found my tongue at last. 'Ruairidh . . . had a fight with Lachie?' I exclaimed. 'What are you talking about, girl?'

She tossed her head haughtily, her long plaits flying. 'I am telling you, Ruairidh had a fight with Lachie,' she repeated stubbornly. 'I never let on to you about it before now, because I knew you would get wild and not believe me.'

She was right there, but I managed to keep my mouth shut for a wonder.

'You mind Lachie was home for a few days at the beginning of the month?' she said.

I nodded.

'Well, he came up here one night, late on. It was a Saturday night. He was going to try the pool below the falls for a salmon. Well, he met Ruairidh. He was prowling about on the top here. Ruairidh told him he was to turn back. Lachie got wild, not seeing why Ruairidh should be guarding the pool for the Laird, just because he was working at the salmon fishing, when the pair of them had poached it together many a night. Anyway, they fought before Lachie would turn back. I wondered about it when he told me, for he was terrible wild at Ruairidh. But I can see it now.'

'See what?' I said stupidly, wanting to take hold of her plaits, and shake sense into her head.

'I can see now that Ruairidh was on the look-out for the smugglers,' she said impatiently. 'What else? Maybe he was not too sure about it. That is why he would never let on to Lachie, in case word got out about it before he was ready. But he had to get Lachie out of the way somehow, so he pretended he was watching the pool for poachers. Poor Lachie got wild at him and there was a fight. But Ruairidh got rid of him in the end.'

I gazed at her admiringly. 'By golly, Catriona, you are not slow,' I said.

'Well, do you believe me now?' she demanded, flushed and triumphant.

'I believe you,' I said, and so I did. Ruairidh would never have come to blows with Lachie, unless that was the only way he could be rid of him without revealing his real reason for being on watch.

'Was it very late on when Lachie met him?' I asked her.

She nodded. 'Aye, it was near the Sabbath. Lachie was away on the Monday, and he wanted to try the pool before he was gone. Don't you let on, mind. There would be an awful row at home, if they got word that Lachie had been out poaching on the Sabbath.'

'You can depend on me,' I said, thinking to myself that there had been more than poaching taking place on the Sabbath. If Ruairidh had been on the look-out from the cliff top, what else could it be but smugglers?

'Is "Morgana" something to do with it?' Catriona asked.

I nodded, my mind busy with the story she had told me. If only Ruairidh had not been such a lone wolf. But that was him all over, treading his own path, never thinking of seeking assistance. If only he had let me know what was going on – a hint just – how much easier it would be now.

'Well, what has "Morgana" got to do with it?' Catriona demanded.

I had been wrong about the numbers in the diary, and it seemed I had been wrong not to think seriously about smuggling, so I was not going to risk making a third blunder. 'I don't know,' I said.

'But you have a good idea,' she persisted.

I admitted that I had an idea about it, and she kept on at me until I said: ' "Morgana" might be the name of a ship.' It sounded better that way than saying she was an old Spanish galleon, the treasure ship of the Armada.

She shook her head, frowning. 'It seems an awful fancy name for a ship,' she said doubtfully. Long John had said much the same thing. 'You could imagine them having a name like that in olden times,' she went on. 'But not now. I doubt you are wrong there, Niall.'

I could not have been more pleased if the Laird had suddenly presented me with a boat, and I was off with Long John for a shot at the shark fishing. But I hugged my secret to myself, not saying a word, and just nodded.

'Are you going to keep a watch for the smugglers?' she said eagerly. 'Maybe they are coming in on the Sabbath. It was a Saturday night, mind, when Lachie came on Ruairidh.'

'I don't know,' I said. There was an awkward pause. I knew the words had not rung true. 'If the Harris man is at the bothy, it is not easy for me to get away without him seeing,' I added lamely.

It was not that I did not trust Catriona, but I was afraid of Morag. She would keep on at Catriona until she had squeezed every scrap of information out of her, and she was a terrible chatterbox. The less she knew the better.

Catriona got to her feet and stuck her nose in the air, the way she did when she was offended. I knew she felt that I did not trust her, so I said quickly: 'Reach over on Sunday after church. If I have any more news, I will tell you then.'

'I'll see,' she said, her nose still in the air, trying to make out she was not all that interested in my news. 'I am not coming on my own, though.'

'You don't have to,' I said, every bit as sharply. 'Morag has legs on her. Let her use them.'

'She may not be able. Your aunt is against walking out on the Sabbath.'

'Ach, to pot with Aunt Phemie,' I said.

'You are bold enough, seeing you are miles away from her,' she said. 'There would be no skipping out for yourself on the Sabbath, let me tell you, if you were at home just now.'

'Well, I am safe enough at the bothy,' I said, not wanting to get wild at her, for fear it would put her off coming. 'Aunt Phemie would never manage the track, that is a sure thing. They would need to roll her down the gorge. Is she still as fat as ever?'

'Fatter.' Catriona giggled, her bad temper forgotten. 'Morag reckons she is near twenty stone.'

'Good life,' I said, 'it is a wonder to me she ever got clear of Africa. If the cannibals had only had a big enough pot, she would have kept them going for long enough.'

Catriona laughed until the tears came to her eyes, and I was so pleased at the success of my joke that I stopped worrying about the height of her. I had been thinking she had grown since I saw her last. She looked even taller, anyway, but I suppose that was nonsense. It was only a few days since I had last seen her, and she could not have shot up in that time. It is bad to worry about things. It makes them far worse.

She wiped her eyes, still laughing, and said: 'You are terrible, Niall.'

'Not as terrible as Aunt Phemie stuck fast in a cannibals' cooking pot,' I said. 'Think of the job they would have hauling her out when she was done.'

That started her off again, and she was still laughing as she collected her bicycle in the old quarry and wheeled it to the road. She was just about to start off when she said: 'I clean forgot to tell you, Donald was in an accident last night.'

'Donald who?' I said, thinking that living in the bothy

at the foot of the gorge was like being shut up in a dungeon, cut off from all sight and sound of the people in our township. That was the only bad thing about it, not knowing what was going on in the place.

'Donald Stewart,' she said. 'He was coming back from Portree in his old car at the time.'

'Good life, was he hurt?' I said. I liked Donald, and he had been more than kind to us since Ruairidh was hurt.

'No, but the other fellow was. He came flying round a corner, Donald said, at an awful speed. He went clean off the road and his car turned over. If it hadn't been for the tent he would have been hurt worse.'

'Tent? What tent?' I said.

'The man had a tent in the back of his car, Donald said. It made a sort of padding when the car turned over. Donald said it was the tent that saved him. But they had to fetch the ambulance.'

She pushed the pedal round and prepared to mount the bicycle. The stranger who had fled from the hidden camp site at the river must have had a tent in his car, I thought. 'Did Donald say what the man looked like?' I said quickly.

'He was a stranger,' Catriona said. 'A tourist. Donald said he got a bad knock on the head, and he was bald, poor man. Not a hair on his head.'

I watched Catriona cycle off down the road. She looked back and waved, and the cycle took a bad wobble. If she was not careful, she would be getting a knock herself. I watched her until she disappeared over the brow of the hill. When she was gone, I walked back slowly to the quarry.

So the stranger's car had gone off the road. He must have been certain that I would make for the police when he had fled with such haste, and driven so recklessly that he had smashed the car. Well, that was one of them out of the way. The red fellow would get a shock when he discovered that his partner was out of action. I wondered what he would do about it.

An old crumbling dyke marked the boundary of the quarry and the cliff top. I made through a gap in the dyke, hands deep in the pockets of my denim trousers.

A familiar voice said: 'It is a good job I am patient, eh?'

I suppose it was because I was thinking about him that I got such a shock. I whirled round as if the point of a sword had been thrust in my back. A tall figure rose up from behind the dyke. It was the red fellow.

Chapter Fourteen

'I was waiting for you,' he said. 'I saw you with the girl when I was making over the top o' the quarry, and I thought I would wait for you.' He paused uncertainly, looking down at his big red hands. 'I thought we might make down to the bothy together.'

So that was it! He was afraid to face Long John by himself. He probably thought it would be easier for him, if he had me at his side. Now that I realized his purpose, I was angry with myself for being scared so easily. I was painfully conscious that he had seen me jump like a frightened girl at the sound of his voice. Being angry with myself, I had to strike out at him.

'What brings you back?' I said, not troubling to hide the contempt in my voice. 'I thought you had cleared off for good.'

'Ach, no,' he said. 'That was all talk just. I was wild, see, and I thought it would learn Long John to be careful, if I made off for a time.'

'Learn Long John?' I said scornfully, seeking to sting him. 'That will be the day, I am telling you. He is not worrying, the same fellow. I never saw him in better form since I started at the fishing.'

'Aye, I believe it would take a lot to worry Long John,' he said mildly. 'I was saying that to Big Willie, telling him it would be a shame just to throw away his bonus, all because of a few words spoken in anger. Long John is not the man to bear a grudge, I said to Willie.'

'Is he coming back?' I asked.

'Aye, Willie will be along in the morning, without fail,' he said.

We had reached the start of the track down to the bridge, and he stood back to let me go in front. I never stirred an inch, making out that I was looking across the Sound, and all the time watching him out of the corner of my eye. To tell the truth, I would not have gone down that track with him at my back for all the treasure ships in creation. He hesitated, and I thought he was about to speak, but he went on ahead without a word.

I followed him down the track, keeping a good distance between us. I had the feeling that his meek manner was a sham, a false cloak that could be stripped off in an instant. Well, if he thought he could catch me by surprise and hurl me down the gorge, he was mistaken. I would be away like the wind before those long arms of his could get near me. But he never even turned his head, and I, for my part, never took my eyes off his back.

Long John must have been watching the track from inside the bothy, because he came out and stood gazing up at us, before we were a quarter of the way down. I felt more secure at the sight of him, and I closed the distance between me and the red fellow. He would not dare to try any tricks with Long John's eyes on him.

Long John was grinning all over his face as we drew near the bothy. 'Well, well, Murdo, so you are back,' he said heartily, giving me a sly wink when the red fellow was not looking. 'It was my cooking you were missing, admit it now. Big Willie is after poisoning you, that is why you are back, eh?'

He teased him unmercifully, shooting quick glances at me whenever he got the chance, as much as to say, we must take care not to make him suspicious. He could say a lot with only a look, Long John.

'And what about Big Willie?' he demanded. 'Have you no word of the bold William?'

'He will be along in the morning,' the red fellow muttered.

Long John slapped him on the back. 'Good on you, Murdo,' he cried, 'and it's myself that is well pleased to have the pair o' you back with me.'

He put a hand on the red fellow's shoulder, in the friendliest fashion, and guided him into the bothy. To see the way he acted, you would never believe that this was the man he was going to report to the police if he had not appeared at the bothy before starting time in the morning. Of course, it was the only way to deal with the red fellow, if he was to get no inkling that we were plotting his downfall.

It would not be so simple with Big Willie. He was not the man to take kindly to a teasing, no matter how good-humoured it might be. But I need not have worried. Long John greeted him in the morning as if nothing had passed between them. He glanced at his bandaged hand and asked if the nurse had dressed it. Big Willie grunted a surly reply.

It was like watching a patient trainer coaxing a suspicious animal out of its shell, to see the cunning way Long John gradually worked the big fellow out of his black mood. Big Willie almost always started the day in a black mood, and it was blacker than ever today, seeing it was less than twenty-four hours since he had left the job, after boldly declaring that he would not be marching back in a hurry.

Long John started by getting him chatting about his cattle – and even the dourest of men will always talk about cattle – and I noticed how slyly he managed to work in a joke or two whenever Willie started moaning about poor prices and looked like getting cross again. From cattle he turned to music, asking Willie about songs that an uncle of his, a famous Gaelic Bard, had made. It is a fine thing to have an uncle who is not only a Bard, but a famous one at that, and I could see the pride swelling in the big fellow, as he talked about the great songs his uncle had made. And when we were laying out the rollers on the rough slip to the river, Long John asked him which nets did he think would be the better for changing. By the time we were out in the coble, Big Willie was a different man from the glowering fellow who had arrived at the bothy on the stroke of eight.

It was an education at the salmon fishing. You could learn more just watching Long John handling his men than you would ever get from a whole roomful of books.

The day was dead calm, just the least whisper of a breeze from a point a shade south of sou'east, and the sun blazed down from a cloudless sky. It was just as well that the weather was good, for we had a hard day before us. There were two days' fishing in all the nets, apart from the Rock net, but you would never have known it by the catch we got. It was not the equal of a normal day, for the heavy swell had kept the fish from coming in.

The gale had left all the nets dirty, even the clean one that we had put out the day before yesterday. Every one of the leader nets was thick with weed, long fronds of the stuff entangled in the mesh. It was going to be some job getting the nets clean again. But the storm had driven the jellyfish away. That was one thing to be thankful for, although they would soon be back if the calm spell lasted.

We put out one set of clean nets and fished all six of them before dinner. Even with the cool air off the sea, we were all soaked in sweat when we came in for our dinner. I had a quick wash in the river, and that cooled me down, but I spoilt it by taking three mugs of tea. I believe I sweated every drop of that tea straight out again, as I was scrubbing the slime off the dirty nets after dinner.

We were carting the dirty nets up to the drying green when the *Kingfisher* was sighted. The nets were heaved off the handbarrows and there was a mad rush to get the boxed salmon down from the store shed to the coble. We got them all aboard in record time, and I was never so glad to get out to sea, away from the blistering heat of the airless gorge.

We lost no time in transferring the catch to the *Kingfisher* and in taking on a fresh supply of ice. 'By golly, we will be needing it, boys, if this weather keeps up,' Long John said, as he dropped back into the coble. His face was running with sweat, and I realized then the effort it must cost him to keep up with the rest of them. But he never complained or shirked any of the work, which he could have done easily enough, seeing he was skipper. It was not in him to think of avoiding work because he moved with a crutch. There was not an idle bone in his body.

We put in again and finished spreading the dirty nets. Then we set out for the Rock net, which had suffered worse than the others in the gale, with a clean bag and leader net. It was good to sit back at the helm, one hand trailing in the water, the other one at the controls. It was a different world from yesterday, the sea as smooth as a sheltered pond, and the air so clear that I could make out the white specks of houses along the coast at Gairloch, far across the Sound.

The sun seemed to have put new life into the men, and I never saw nets changed with the speed that the clean leader and bag were rigged at the Rock net. The dirty nets were heavy with a tangled mass of weed, and my arms knew all about the weight of it by the time I had finished helping to haul them aboard. A whole length of spunyarn had been rubbed off the rope of the leader net, where the swell had ground it against the rocks and the rope itself had started to fray.

'There is a good price to be had for the salmon, boy,' Long John said, as he examined the frayed rope, 'but the cost o' fresh gear is not long in eating into the profits.'

Nobody spoke on the way back to the river, but I felt we were none the worse for that. It was the sort of day when you had no need of talk. There were noises enough for company; the steady beat of the engine, the soft splash of the tide against the coble, and the cries of the swooping gulls. Indeed, there was something about the day that held you silent, in the way that even an empty church will still a noisy tongue.

The sea was so calm you could trace the course of the underwater currents as they cut long swathes across the still surface. The cliffs towered straight from the blue water, stretching as far south as the eye could see, broken only by the deep cut of the gorge. It was as if a giant's axe had hacked a huge piece out of that great wall of rock.

I took the coble into the river mouth and there was none of the anxious glances I had noticed the first time Long John had let me take her in alone. As I cut the engine, and nosed the coble into the berth below the bothy, Big Willie said cheerily : 'I am as dry as a cork just. Away and make tea, boy. The rest of us will see to the nets.'

I had the tea waiting when they came back from the drying green, but they hauled up the coble before stopping to take it. Long John took out his old silver watch and squinted down at it. 'Near eight o'clock, boys,' he said. 'By golly, we made up for yesterday.'

Big Willie sipped his hot tea noisily. 'The time has fairly passed,' he said. 'I never noticed the going of it. Supposing the weather is good, it is a pleasure working.'

'Aye, it was a topper of a day,' the red fellow added.

'Well, we made the most of it,' Long John said. 'A grand day's work just.' He glanced across at me. 'But the fellow in the corner is silent. Maybe we have scunnered him with work, boys. He is near done by the look of him, anyway.'

'I am tired, right enough,' I said, smiling. 'But I enjoyed it fine.'

'You did well,' Long John said. He winked broadly. 'I was thinking of getting you to scrub out the bothy on the Sabbath, but seeing you have done your fair share I am letting you off. You can make home for the week-end. Willie will give you a lift.'

'Aye, and welcome,' the big fellow said.

I finished my tea and went outside, hoping that Long John would follow. But he was laughing and joking with the other two, and showed no sign of making a move. I was deeply angry with him, caught in the grip of a sudden jealousy. Why should he be talking so warmly with Big Willie and the red fellow, whilst I, who shared so much with him, stood outside the bothy, alone and disregarded? It was a foolish notion and it passed as quickly as it came. What on earth would the red fellow think if he saw Long John and me whispering together on our own?

I moved away from the bothy, and sprawled out on the grass between the fresh water spring and the river. Now that I was lying full length, the empty feeling of utter weariness left me. I felt an almost pleasant ache in every limb, the cool grass against my hot body gave me a feeling of well-being. What with the heat of the sun on my face, and the soft murmur of the river, and the cry of the sea-birds, I very near drifted off to sleep.

Long John came out of the bothy at last, but Big Willie and the red fellow were hard on his heels. You would never think that they had been at his throat only yester-day. The three of them were chatting together as if they had never known a cross word between them.

Big Willie moved away from the other two and strode across to me. 'Time for off, boy,' he said.

I sat up and stretched, hoping he would walk on. 'I doubt I will never manage the gorge,' I said, yawning. 'I am as stiff as a board just.'

'Good life, when I was your age I would make up the gorge on my hands,' he exclaimed. 'Get moving, boy.' He marched on and I got to my feet as Long John reached me.

He put a hand on my shoulder and said softly: 'Bring the diary on Monday. We will see if you missed anything in it. Don't worry, I will keep a sharp eye on the bold Murdo.'

'But . . .' I started. I clamped my mouth shut again. The red fellow was coming up quickly behind us.

Big Willie had reached the bridge. He glanced over his shoulder, and shouted: 'Are you coming, boy?'

'Aye, coming,' I yelled.

The red fellow was standing alongside Long John now. He was looking pleased with himself, I thought. He stuck out his long neck and said: 'See and have a good weekend, boy.' His cold eyes met mine briefly. 'Tell your mother I was asking for Ruairidh.'

'Aye, I will tell her,' I said, hoping my voice did not betray my feelings.

I glanced at Long John and caught his sly wink, no more

than the flicker of an eyelid. But it was enough for me. I smiled at him and ran after Big Willie.

I caught up with him on the other side of the bridge. 'Good life,' he grunted, 'I thought you were never coming.'

But he was in no hurry, judging by the speed of him. He plodded up the track at such a crawl that I felt like pushing him aside, and getting in front. I could have waited until he was near the top, and still reached the quarry before he got his motor-bike started.

When he did get her started I said: 'Willie, I don't think I will go home after all. Aunt Phemie is staying at the house, and you know what she is like.'

She had once come upon him chasing sheep out of his ripe corn, cursing and bawling at them for ruining his crop, and she had given him an awful dressing down for his language. Willie had never forgotten it.

He throttled down the engine and looked at me with concern. 'Good life, I would sooner take to the heather than stay in the house with that old warrior,' he said. 'You are wise to keep clear, boy, until she is away. But you could have saved yourself the climb.'

'Ach, I am the better for it,' I said, delighted that he had accepted my excuse so readily.

'It is as well you spoke,' he said, frowning. 'I am not going near your house, not even to ask for poor Ruairidh, as long as that woman is there. You have no idea, boy, the tongue she has on her.'

He had such a comical look on his face that I had a job not to burst out laughing. 'Oh, I know fine,' I said solemnly. 'Don't you worry. Morag will get word to me about Ruairidh.'

The frown left Big Willie's face. He beamed. 'Aye. Fine.' He raised his bandaged hand. 'See you on Monday then.'

As soon as he had gone, I made for the cliff top, keeping well away from the side of the gorge. I lowered myself over the edge of the cliff, and climbed down to the clump of bushes on the lip of the overhang. The thick branches of the centre bush formed a Y. I wedged my feet against them, my back to the cliff. Shielded by the leafy branches I settled down to wait.

I had intended to let Long John know of my plan but I had not got a chance to speak to him alone. Perhaps it was just as well, for I had a feeling that he would not have approved of it. That was the trouble, now that I had got him firmly on my side he would want to plan everything himself, and I would become no more than an idle spectator.

There was a haze over the Sound. The hills of the mainland had disappeared behind a thick wall of cottonwool clouds. Far to the north, a fog hooter blared out in the Minch. There was a sea mist creeping in, a sure sign of good weather at this time of year, but the worst thing that could have happened from my point of view.

At first I had been glad of the leafy shade of the bushes, but I soon started to chill. I could not have been there more than an hour or so when I started to get cramp in my legs. I tried bending them, one at a time, but I could not keep the cramp at bay.

The sea mist was coming in fast. Directly below me I could still see a patch of clear water, but great clouds of thick white vapour were rolling up to the river mouth, and drifting into the gorge.

It may have been the mist blanketing my view, or my cramped position under the bushes; whatever it was I felt as if time had come to a standstill. It seemed not only hours, but days since I had parted from Big Willie in the quarry. I was lost in a strange half-world, suspended between land and sea, it seemed, in a mist-shrouded world of absolute silence. I strained my ears for the sound of oars or an engine, but I could not hear a thing.

I think it was an insect that had got down my back, for I had a sudden, terrible itch between my shoulder blades. I twisted round to scratch it the better. Out of the corner of my eye I saw something move.

I pushed myself up out of the bushes, feeling my legs weak and helpless, and flattened round against the cliff. It was the red fellow. He was climbing carefully down the cliff towards me. My stomach turned to water. I stared up at him immovable as a rabbit before a ferret.

He had his back to the cliff face, and he was letting himself down only inches at a time. With every step he dug his heels in firmly, and he had his hands spread wide to brake himself if he slipped. He was looking around for footholds, and he did not see me at first. When he saw me watching him, he stopped.

We stared at each other for a long time, neither of us moving. He never said a word, just drew in his bottom lip on his stained teeth, and stared at me. There was no need for him to speak. I could see all I needed to know on his face, and the sight of it made me tremble. With his eyes still on my face, he started to edge down the cliff towards me.

As he moved, I snapped out of my trance. I climbed up out of the bushes and moved awkwardly to the right, my legs feeling as if they did not belong to me. He worked across to his left, to cut me off. I stopped, panting, realizing that I would be within his reach before I could gain the safety of the cliff top.

He took a hissing breath, his teeth bared, and started to move down towards me again. It was his silence that unnerved me more than anything, and he had covered half the distance between us before I could summon my trembling body to move.

I scrambled away to my left, as quickly as I dared. That stopped his downward movement. He worked his way along, trying to keep pace with me and bar my path to the cliff top. I twisted suddenly in the opposite direction, and started to scramble wildly up the cliff face. My foot slipped, and I caught at a tuft of grass. It came away in my hand. I slid down, clawing at the unyielding ground.

I felt a branch whip against my face, and I snatched at it desperately. It slid through my fingers. The cliff was no longer beneath me. I was falling through space.

I can remember thinking, stupidly, but this can't be happening to me.

Chapter Fifteen

In the last fear-stricken fraction of a second, as I glimpsed the up-rushing sea through the swirling clouds of mist, I automatically did the one thing that was the saving of me. I stiffened my outstretched arms and held my body rigid, so that when I struck the water I did so in a clean dive. Had it not been for that last second movement, my body would have been smashed by the force of the fall.

I think I must have been stunned as I struck the water, for I have no recollection of my downward dive from that moment on. I remembered no more until I found myself floating on the surface, racked with coughing, as I tried to get the salt water out of my lungs.

I was no more than half-conscious. I arched up in the water, coughing and choking, arms flailing wildly, striking out in panic I knew not where. It was the worst thing I could have done. My small reserve of strength was soon spent. My threshing arms grew still. I gave a last feeble kick and sank beneath the surface.

Down, down, down. Down into the cold, dark depths below the cliffs, lost in a green, sunless world from which there was no escape. Down, down, down, until I thought my aching lungs must surely burst. It was the sense of not being able to touch bottom that was the worst horror of all, the awful feeling of sinking helplessly into a bottomless pit.

There was a hammer beating inside my skull. Great weights were pressing on my chest. Another second and my lungs must burst. I kicked out desperately and shot to the surface.

As I broke water, my outstretched hands struck something solid. It was a cork float, coated with slime. My clawing fingers slid off it and fastened around the thick rope of the leader net. I hung on grimly. I had my head down and the water poured from my open mouth. Choking and sobbing, retching with the salt water in my lungs, I gasped for air.

After a while I let go of the rope with my left hand, and lay on my back. A wash of water broke over my face and started another fit of coughing. I got over it and lay still again. My only thought was to suck air into my straining lungs, and rest my bruised and battered body.

The mist lay all around, only a few feet from the surface of the water. I could make out the dark base of the cliff on either side of the leader net, but that was all. Far out in the Minch I could hear the regular hooting of a fog siren.

I shifted my hold on the rope. Somehow or other I had to get ashore before cold and tiredness overcame me and I lost my grip. If I went under again I knew full well that I would never return to the surface alive.

I had already lost one gumboot, and now I kicked off the other one. I rolled over, seizing the rope with both hands, and kicking out with my legs. Moving one hand over the other, I started to work towards the shore.

I was so weak that I had to stop and rest every few feet of the way. Every time I started afresh, the effort to move seemed greater than the time before. But I drew steadily nearer the dark bulk of the cliff, and that gave me new heart. When I reached the land stick at the end of the rope, I hung on to it, panting, drawing in great sobbing breaths of air. I gazed stupidly at the sheer face of the cliff only a few feet away, my heart sinking as I stared at it. I had forgotten that the tide was high. The shelf of rock at the base of the cliff, which formed a buttress all the way to the river, was deep under water except at low tide.

I tightened my grip on the land stick. It was held in place by a rope bridle. The bridle was attached to a short length of chain that was fastened to a rock pin sunk in the cliff above the ledge. The rock pin, too, was under water.

I thought of shouting for help but who would hear me? My cries would never carry the length of the bothy, and Long John had no reason to be out looking for me. As far as he was concerned I was safely at home for the week-end. The only man who might hear me, if he was still prowling around the cliff top, was the red fellow. And he was the last man to come to my aid.

I gazed up at the cliff face, seeing the band of wet rock where the tide had started to ebb. It was only inches below the high tide mark, so it could not have been long on the turn. It would take another hour or two before the ledge emerged from the water. I shifted my grip from the greasy land stick back to the rope, and prepared to wait.

It was a long wait, and my strength ebbed faster than the tide. I was so cold now that I could not stop my teeth chattering, and I began to imagine that my numbed fingers were slipping off the rope. The thought brought terror and renewed strength. I took a fresh grip and threshed the water with my legs, stubbing my toe on an unyielding rock. The cry I gave was one of joy, for I could see the dark outline of the shelving rock only a few feet below me. The rock pin and a few links of dripping chain were already clear of the sea.

I pulled myself up on the rope bridle, my feet wedged against the sloping outcrop of rock. Shifting my grip to the short chain, I heaved myself up out of the water and crawled against the cliff. My head and shoulders were out of the water and I hung on to the chain with both hands lest the pull of the ebb tide should sweep me from my perch. With my back to the cliffs, more dead than alive, I waited for the tide to drop.

It was when I tried to get to my feet that I realized how far through I was. I was shivering uncontrollably all over, and I seemed to have lost command of my limbs. I fell twice before I managed to get to my feet, and I moved like a drunken man.

Some stretches of the ledge were of smooth, flat rock, but there were others where the surface was pitted and broken, and the feet of my stockings were soon in shreds. In two places there was a narrow gap in the ledge where the sea lapped darkly below. I had to nerve myself to jump these gaps, and I came to grief at the second of them, slipping and falling heavily. I lay where I had fallen, too sick and dizzy to move. When I put my hand up to my head it came away wet with blood.

I tried to get to my feet, but I could not rise beyond my knees. One hand in a shallow pool, and the other deep in a patch of slippery weed, I strained forward, my body racked with vomiting. The spasm passed. I got up, and staggered on.

It was a nightmare journey, slipping and falling on the wet, weed-strewn shelf of rock, cut and bruised and miserably cold, forcing one weary leg after the other, blindly determined to reach the shelter of the bothy and Long John.

When I came to the river mouth, the way was barred by a mass of fallen boulders, but I climbed round them and made my way up the side of the gorge to the bridge. The mist was thicker than ever in the gorge, and I almost missed the track leading to the bridge. But I righted myself in time and stumbled on. It never occurred to me that I might slip and plunge into the river far below. Now that I had come so far, and endured so much, I felt that I could not fail.

I forced myself up the narrow catwalk and fell across the bridge exhausted, my arms locked around the narrow planks. Looking down, it was as if a huge fire of wet wood had been lit in the gorge. The mist swirled under the bridge like smoke, blotting out the river below and the far bank. The muffled roar of the falls, the noise of the swift-flowing river, and the faint hooting of a fog siren far out in the Minch, echoed eerily through the thick white vapour.

I crawled across the bridge on my hands and knees, and tumbled down the ladder at the other side. Picking myself up, I staggered on down the river bank.

The beached coble loomed up out of the mist like a crouching dragon ready to spring. It gave me such a start that I half fell across the square stern. I rested against it, peering through the mist at the dim outline of the bothy, the small window a pale yellow eye in the gloom.

There was a sudden outburst of angry voices, the one shouting the other down. The voices stopped suddenly, and I heard a man's terrified scream. I stumbled towards the lighted window of the bothy.

The lantern was standing on the end of the table, casting its light on the red fellow. He was pressed back against the wall, his right arm held up to shield his face. The blood dripped from an open gash across his cheek, and if ever I saw fear, I saw it on him, stamped plain on every line of his face. And no wonder. Long John was standing in the centre of the room, his ebony handled knife balanced flat on the palm of his hand, his arm flexed ready for the throw.

If the face of the Harris man was ugly with fear, the look that Long John had was ugly, too. But it was anger that twisted his face, not fear. I had never before seen a man in the grip of such a rage, and I hope I never will again.

'Make what noise you will, Murdo,' he thundered. 'Only the walls of the bothy can hear you, and your whining will not move them. It would take all the trumpets of Jehovah to bring down these walls about my ears.'

The red fellow mumbled something, his bulging eyes fixed on the gleaming blade of the knife.

Long John leaned forward, and there was something wolfish in the way he drew his lips back from his teeth. 'What has it profited you to silence the boy, when I am here to settle the score?' he said. 'You have not much time left, Murdo. Time to make a little prayer just. Time for that, and no more.'

I do not remember opening my mouth, but I must have made some sound, for the pair of them swung round to the window. Long John slowly lowered his knife. His face was a study, blank astonishment and deep concern struggling to gain the mastery.

The red fellow let out a sort of strangled moan. If there had been fear on his face as he had cowered back from Long John, it was nothing to the look he had now. His legs started to buckle. He moaned again, and slid slowly to the floor.

Long John threw the door of the bothy wide open. I staggered inside. He gripped me by the shoulders. If it had not been for his firm clasp, I believe I would have fallen to the floor like the red fellow. 'Good life, boy, I thought you were done for,' he said, his dark eyes anxiously searching my face.

I tried to speak, but my teeth were chattering so hard that I could not get the words out. He pushed me over to the fire. 'Off with those clothes,' he ordered.

I stripped off my sodden clothes, keeping a wary eye on the red fellow. He was slumped on the floor, his head lolling on his chest. The blood from the cut on his cheek was making a dark stain on his jersey. His eyes were closed.

'He has seen his first ghost,' Long John said grimly. 'I doubt the sight of it has very near finished him.'

He set to work, rubbing me down vigorously with a dry towel. When he had done, he pulled a thick flannel shirt over my head. It was one of his own, and I must have looked a queer sight in it, for it came down below my knees. But I made no move to protest. Now that I had reached my goal, all my remaining strength seemed to have drained from my limbs. I could only stand there, dazed and shivering, thankful that I need not lift a finger to help myself.

'It is the bunk for you, boy,' he said. 'You are all in.'

So I was. I could not stop shivering, and it was as much as I could do to keep my eyes open. Indeed, I might well have been sleep-walking, for what was happening held no more reality for me than a dream.

Long John had made up a bed for me in the bottom bunk below his own. I crawled in thankfully between the rough blankets, and he handed me a mug. 'Drink that,' he urged.

I took a sip and shuddered, as the fiery liquor burned my throat.

'Put it down in one swallow,' he said, 'like a right fisherman. It will make you sleep.'

I swallowed it obediently, and got such a fit of coughing

that I was afraid I would bring it straight up again. Long John took the mug from me and patted my shoulder. 'A good sleep will put you right, Niall,' he said gently. 'We will deal with the red fellow in the morning.'

He shut the door behind him, and I rolled over on my side. I think it was rum he had given me, and I could feel it warming my stomach, but I was asleep before I had time to think much about it.

It was a disturbed sleep that I had. I imagined that I could hear the throb of a diesel engine, and the creak of ghostly rowlocks, and the sound of strange voices, and the shrill note of a queer, high-pitched laugh. I thought I was still dreaming when I awoke to the sound of that laugh.

I sat up in the bunk, rubbing my eyes. Daylight filtered into the room through the small, dirty window. Once again I heard that high-pitched laugh, and the sound of strange voices. They came from the other side of the wooden partition. I glanced across at the red fellow's bunk. It had not been slept in. I strained my ears. There was a murmur of voices from the other room. Strange voices.

'John,' I called hesitantly. 'John MacGregor.'

The voices were silent. Slow footsteps approached the door. It was pushed open, and a big, red-faced man looked in at me. He tossed my clothes on the bunk and went out again before I had time to open my mouth.

I threw my clothes on, wondering who he was and what had happened to Long John. Although it was daylight the air was chill, and I guessed it must be very early in the morning. I pulled on the socks that the big man had thrown in with my clothes. They were much too big for me. Long John's, I supposed. I tucked my trousers inside them and opened the door to the kitchen. I stopped dead in my tracks. Long John was not there.

'Come on in, son,' the big, red-faced man said. He was sitting at the end of the table, sipping rum out of a mug. An open bottle was standing at his elbow. A young fellow with a thin, sharp face was lounging with his back to the fire. He was not many years older than me by the look of him, and he needed a haircut.

'What have you got to say for yourself, Harry?' the big man said. 'That is the sprat that put you to flight at Broadford. What do you say to that, eh?' He let out the queer, high-pitched laugh I had heard before.

The fellow called Harry scowled at the two of us in turn. 'It was the mist,' he said. 'Do you suppose I would have run from a boy that size, if I had seen him right?'

'Are you the one who made off with my brother's clothes from the hospital?' I said hotly, my fists clenching.

Before he had a chance to reply, the red fellow ducked his long frame under the stone lintel. He strode across to the table and took a swig from the bottle of rum. He corked it and put the bottle in his pocket. 'So you are up,' he said, turning to me. 'Well, we can get moving.'

I had taken a step back at the sight of him, but now I came forward again. 'What have you done with Long John?' I demanded.

He took no heed of me, saying to the big man: 'Watch him, Duncan. There will be trouble with the boss if he gives us the slip.'

As he ducked out of the bothy I made to go after him, but the big man caught me by the arm. 'Wait for me, son,' he said, draining his mug in one gulp. He was beaming at me, and he had spoken in the friendliest way, but there was nothing friendly about the way he held my arm. I tried to wrench myself free, but the thin fellow seized my other arm and I was forced out of the door between them.

The mist was rising slowly from the gorge, but I could not see as far as the river mouth on the one hand, or the bridge on the other. The red fellow was at the oars of a dinghy, and the big man dragged me into the stern with him. The thin fellow pushed off, and leapt into the bows.

'Where are we going?' I asked, and I could not keep the tremor out of my voice.

None of them spoke. The red fellow pulled strongly on the starboard oar, and swung the dinghy round downstream.

'You will pay for this when Long John hears of it,' I said, trying to speak confidently.

The red fellow's pale eyes looked into mine. There was venom in them. 'You can forget about Long John,' he said. 'And shut up.'

I swallowed. The big man squeezed the muscles of my arm until I almost cried out in pain. 'The man says shut up,' he murmured. I gritted my teeth. He nodded approvingly, slowly relaxing the pressure on my arm.

There was silence. The only sound came from the creaking of the rowlocks. A boat loomed up out of the mist, a fishing boat lying at anchor in the river mouth. She was a dirty brown, and looked as if she had not seen a lick of paint in years. The glass was broken in the window on the port side of her square wheelhouse, and a piece of hardboard had been jammed in from the inside to keep out the weather.

As we came alongside, the first of my foolish dreams turned to dust. I saw her name, not in letters of gold, but in dirty white paint. The letters were chipped and peeling, and not easy to read, but I spelled out the name all right. The fishing boat was called *Morgana*.

Chapter Sixteen

A stocky, grey-haired man, wearing a much-darned fisherman's jersey, was leaning over the side of the fishing boat. He handed me up on deck and the big man and the red fellow clambered aboard quickly behind me.

I tripped over a buckled metal plate on the foredeck. The red fellow caught my arm and pushed me down a wooden ladder. The door to the crew's quarters was open. I caught a glimpse of a bare wooden table, and bunks on either side. If the big man spread his elbows, there would not be much room for the rest of them.

There was another door on my left. The red fellow

opened it a little and put his head inside. I heard him mutter: 'The boy's here.' He stepped back and another hand propelled me forward. I tripped over the step, and the door closed behind me.

I was standing inside a tiny cabin, only the length of the narrow bunk on the opposite wall, and not more than twice its width. Long John was lying on the bunk. He looked up at me, unsmiling. 'Welcome to *Morgana*,' he said.

My mind may have grown fuddled for want of rest, or it may have been that I had come to depend upon him as my friend, and the image of a good friend cannot change to that of an enemy in the blink of an eye. Whatever the reason, I stared at him blankly, not grasping the significance of his words. He soon put me straight.

'Well, boy, you beat me in the end,' he said. 'I thought the first night in the bothy would have finished you, but no. You had to come back for more, eh?' He sighed. 'If only you had cleared off at the start, you would have saved me many a headache – aye, and saved yourself a packet o' trouble, too.'

Even then I could not – or would not – accept what he had to say. 'But . . . but it was the red fellow who tried to scare me off,' I stammered. 'You laid into him that night. You hit him.'

'Because he put his big paws around your neck,' he said quietly. 'He had done enough damage, the same fellow, without starting on you.'

'But what about the day he was not wanting to make out in the coble?' I cried. 'Himself and Big Willie. You were wild at them. Willie very near struck you.'

'A bit of an act, boy,' he said coolly. 'I always fancied myself as a bit of an actor. That was for your benefit. You were the one who should have made for home when you saw the sort of day I was wanting to make out on.'

'But when we got back in with the coble,' I said, dazed and bewildered, unable to believe that he could have done such a thing to me. 'Big Willie and the red fellow – they walked out on you.'

'Aye, poor Willie was that wild he could have been talked into anything, and I had the red fellow talk him into walking out,' he said calmly. 'When the two of them marched off, I thought you would go along with them.'

'But you threw a knife at him,' I said, my head spinning, remembering how the red fellow's eyes had bulged at the quivering blade, how he had stood staring at it, the sweat dripping from his face. 'That was no act. You might have killed him.'

'Aye, I might,' he said slowly. 'But the bold Murdo put his hands on you, mind. I had warned him about that, and I get wild when people cross me.' He smiled suddenly. 'It was myself was the foolish one, eh? You liked seeing Murdo getting a bad scare. It was the knife-throwing that stopped you going with him.'

'It was not,' I said hotly. 'I was sorry for you just. I thought they were letting you down. I . . .' I stopped short, biting my lip. I was the one who had been let down, not him. The man I had taken for a friend had been making a fool of me all the time. The thought made me squirm. I felt my cheeks flaming. 'You must have had a good laugh at me,' I burst out.

He shook his head. 'No laughs. Not one. Headaches just.'

I could almost forgive him all the tricks he had played upon me, all except one. If he had been working hand in glove with the red fellow, it meant that he had lied about not seeing him on the bridge when Ruairidh fell. I said as much to him, and all the fury I felt at my own foolishness fired the words I used.

I thought he would be stung to anger, or try to deny it, but he only said: 'Aye, Murdo was on the bridge with Ruairidh, but there is more to it than that.'

I looked at him suspiciously. When you have once caught out a man in a lie, no matter for what reason, the chances are you will not take his word on the weather, never mind anything else.

'I don't blame you for scowling at me, boy,' he said, 'but I am telling the truth. Ruairidh had been watching us. We knew that. Every Saturday he made out he was away to see a friend of his, a shepherd who stays over the hill, but the Saturday before he had his accident, Murdo saw him spying on us.'

'So he pushed him off the bridge,' I said quickly, 'and you lied to me about it.' That was something I could never forgive him.

'Easy, easy,' he said mildly. 'I am not a man for lies, boy. I take my chances, right enough, and maybe the law would have something to say about that, but my tongue is straight enough whatever.'

The cabin started to vibrate as the diesel engine sprang to life. I heard the anchor being hauled up, and the note of the engine deepen as the boat got under way. 'Well?' I said.

'Murdo got nervous,' he said. 'The same fellow may be handy enough at chasing the likes o' you, but he is as jittery as an old wife when it comes to the bit. The day Ruairidh made off for cigarettes, the bold Murdo thought he was away to the Laird, or the police. He made after your brother, and tackled him on the bridge. Said he had been spying on us, the fool, and that he must know what Ruairidh was about, or it would be the worse for him.'

'Ruairidh is a man with a quick temper, and he took it bad. He told the red fellow straight to his face that he had all the evidence written down that he needed, and that it was the jail for him. He made to go. Murdo pulled him back. The two of them struggled, and Ruairidh fell. That was the way of it.'

'That is enough for me,' I said. 'Aye, and it will be enough for the police, too, once I get word to them.'

'Easy, easy,' he said again. 'Less of the scowling, boy. Good life, it was not me who was on the bridge with Ruairidh. I am the one who hauled him out of the river, when it would have been easy enough to stand aside and see him drown.'

'Aye, but you should have told me,' I said doggedly.

'And have you make off to the police?'

'Why not?' I said, adding boldly: 'The red fellow would be safer in jail, once Ruairidh is out of hospital, and fit to

176

lay hands on him.'

'The red fellow is not the only one to think of,' he said.

'Well, you should have told me,' I persisted.

'What had been done was done,' he said flatly. 'What would it profit poor Ruairidh if I were to rot in a cell? Have sense, boy. It was the jail for me, and I have no fancy for prison bars, let me tell you. I must sniff the sea, or I am done, and sniff it I will, to the last.'

'Why was it the jail for you?' I said. It was a stupid question, I can see that now, but I had still not guessed the purpose of *Morgana*.

'I will tell you, boy,' he said, and I will say that for him, rogue though he may have been, he was the most open man I ever knew. 'This is the way of it. Six days a week I have fished the nets for the Laird, and fished them well, let me tell you. But on the seventh day I have fished them for myself.'

So that was it! *Salmon poaching*! So much for all my wild dreams of sunken Spanish treasure. But salmon poaching on a tremendous scale. Not the odd fish taken from a pool on the river, in the dark of night, and hurried home to the pot, but salmon by the hundred, bringing in hundreds of pounds in return. And it had been right under my nose all the time! I had been handling salmon every day in the week without realizing the worth of them.

'Does it surprise you, boy?' he said. 'It shouldn't. There is money in the salmon poaching the way I have been working it – aye, big money – but it is finished now.' He smiled crookedly. 'If I were the Laird I believe I would give you a gold watch, one wi' your name on it. You have earned it.'

'You were bound to be caught in the end,' I said, never stopping to think how few men would have taken it like that, or feeling any need to watch my tongue with him.

'No fear,' he declared. 'Who was to see us working the nets at dawn on the Sabbath? I had it well planned, boy. The *Morgana* was working out from Gairloch at lobsters and herring all week. She would slip across here on the Saturday night and we would fish the nets at dawn on the

Sabbath.' He chuckled. 'You have heard the saying – the better the day, the better the deed? Well, many a good haul we got for our Sunday work.'

'Then the *Morgana* would make for Kyle, and the boys sold whatever they had in the way o' lobsters or herring to the fish merchants. That way there was no talk. They had a good reason to be in Kyle every week. And it is a short trip up Loch Alsh to Loch Duich, boy. A lonely loch – Duich. Fine for the job, just. A van would be waiting for them on a track by the lochside. Six hours later the Laird's salmon were being sold in Glasgow. Oh, we could have kept at it for long enough, had it not been for you – and the red fellow.'

'The red fellow?' I said, surprised.

He nodded. 'He is all nerves, the same fellow. He thinks you will make for the police, and that would be bad for Murdo. And it would be bad for you, if you are not put out of his reach.'

'Well, what are you going to do about it?' I said defiantly.

He reached out for his crutch and fingered it, and I thought once more how like an old pirate he was with his thick, black hair and lined, weathered face.

'I am going to put you ashore on one of the Crowlin Islands,' he said. 'There are no people staying on them, but you will find a house or two still standing, and I will give you food and blankets. When I am ready, I will send word to your folk.'

'It is as well for you to give in now,' I said. 'The police will find you for sure, and it will be the worse for you in the end.'

He swung off the bunk and tucked his crutch under his arm. 'To pot with the police,' he said. 'Between Red Point and the Summer Isles there are a hundred bays where a man might lie up for the rest of his days, and the police never come near. Or I might make over to Ireland. I always had a fancy for the Galway coast.'

He got up and pointed to the door. 'There is a bolt on the door,' he said. 'Lock it when I am gone. I am taking no more chances with you and the red fellow.'

'Where are we heading for now?' I asked.

'The Crowlins.' He chuckled. 'And when we have you safely ashore, we are off to Loch Duich with the Laird's salmon.'

He had his good leg outside the cabin when I said: 'Was it *Morgana* you had at the shark fishing?'

He turned slowly. 'Aye, it was *Morgana*,' he said. 'The plate of the harpoon gun is on her deck still.'

'I know,' I said. 'I tripped over it when I came aboard.'

'It has been there a long time,' he said. 'It is changed days now for *Morgana*, but that is the way of it.' He turned away, calling over his shoulder: 'Mind you bolt the door.'

I slid the bolt home as he closed the door, and sat down on the bunk. I had only the sketchiest idea of the where-abouts of the Crowlin Islands. They lay somewhere to the south, off the mainland, as far as I knew. I wished I had asked him before he had gone.

It was the thought of how my mother would take my sudden disappearance that worried me. She had enough on her mind already. Besides, I had no fancy to be stranded on one of a group of deserted islands. Supposing Long John had no intention of sending word home. I might be on the island for weeks before I was picked up.

I got up and slid back the bolt softly. I opened the door a crack and put my ear to it. I could hear someone snor-ing loudly.

Long John had said they were making for Loch Duich with the Laird's salmon, after they had got rid of me at the Crowlins, so that meant they must have fished the nets at daybreak. If that was the case, I doubted if any of them had seen their bunks last night. Perhaps they were all sleeping now, with only one man at the wheel. I edged the door open and peeped out.

Somebody yawned on the other side of the door to the crew's quarters. I darted back inside the cabin, hearing a door open. There was another yawn. Footsteps went past the cabin. The wooden ladder creaked. Then silence again, only the steady throb of the diesel. I pressed my ear to the crack of the door, and waited.

The wooden ladder creaked again. Heavy footsteps went past the cabin. A door opened and shut. Perhaps Long John had changed the helmsman, and this was the man who had been relieved returning to his bunk. I waited until my impatience got the better of me. I opened the door an inch at a time and peered out.

The door to the crew's quarters was closed. The snoring was louder than ever. There seemed to be two of them at it now. I stepped out of the cabin and closed the door quietly behind me.

Two strides took me to the wooden ladder and I was up it in a flash. When I reached the level of the deck I raised my head cautiously and chanced a quick glance at the wheelhouse. Harry, the thin-faced fellow, was at the helm. He was looking out of the starboard window, and he suddenly bobbed down and disappeared from view.

I kept my eyes on the wheelhouse. Several minutes passed before he popped up again and took another quick look around. When he disappeared again, I realized that he must be sitting down behind the wheel. I took a deep breath. It was now or never.

I scrambled out on deck and ran swiftly to the port side of the wheelhouse. I made no sound in my stockinged feet and I crouched down against the gunwale. Unless he opened the wheelhouse door he could not see me, because the window on the port side was boarded up.

I shifted my position and felt something sharp against my knee. It was Long John's salmon club. I picked it up and stepped across to the wheelhouse. Now that the time had come to act, I hesitated. But I told myself that the man at the wheel was the fellow who had tried to steal Ruairidh's clothes. That hardened me. I rapped on the door.

It swung open and the thin-faced fellow poked his head out. He was whistling. The whistling stopped suddenly when he saw me, but his lips were still pursed as I hit him with the club. He flopped forward like a sack of meal.

I dragged him out of the wheelhouse and dumped him

against the gunwale. He never made a sound. I darted inside and seized the wheel. For the first time since I had come on deck, I had a look around.

There was a rocky shore on the starboard side, the mist lying low on the land. I pushed the door open and had a look out to port. Nothing there but an open stretch of water, sealed by a thick white mist. I had no idea of the boat's position, but Long John had said we were making for the Crowlin Islands, so we must be heading south. And if the Crowlins were close to the mainland, then the course from the gorge would have taken us through the narrows between the islands of Rona and Raasay, so that land I could see must be the eastern shore of Raasay.

I spun the wheel, bringing *Morgana* round in a wide circle. The sea was dead calm, and she hardly lifted as she met the wash of the tide. There was no danger of anyone below sensing the change of course. I opened the throttle lever a little more, and peered ahead.

I had been right in my reckoning. Dead ahead I could see the narrows between Raasay and Rona, the curving tail of Raasay almost linked to the smaller island of Rona. I followed the curving tail of Raasay, hugging the coast, and as *Morgana* turned into the narrows, I saw the tiny island of Eilean Tigh that marked the western side of the channel.

I opened the throttle lever as far as it would go and headed her into the centre of the channel. I knew that the water was deep here, but the rocky shores of the islands loomed perilously close, and I could see the wash of the currents around the dark reefs. I tightened my grip on the wheel and peered anxiously ahead.

There was a crash as the wheelhouse door slammed back on its hinges. The thin-faced fellow stood in the opening. His face was white, and a trickle of blood smeared his forehead. Without a word he leapt at me.

The force of his rush took me back against the far wall. His hands came up for my throat, but I twisted back and got a bear hug on him. We grappled together, crashing from one side of the wheelhouse to the other, the wheel spinning unheeded, as the pull of the currents moved the rudder.

Although he was taller than me, there was not much weight in him, and I believe I was the stronger. But in the confined space of the wheelhouse I could not get the advantage of him, and he was a dirty fighter. I thought I had him when I swung him round and forced him back over the compass mounting. But he got his fingers inside the corner of my mouth and I had to release him or he would have torn my lip. Before I could get a fresh grip he caught me a stunning blow on the side of the head. I stumbled back against the spinning wheel, getting the spokes in the small of my back.

There was a noise like sheets of stiff brown paper being ripped in two. *Morgana* heeled steeply to port. The door of the wheelhouse swung open as I struck out blindly at the thin fellow. I caught him in the chest. He staggered back through the open door and pitched against the gunwale.

There was a fearful grinding noise and the boat rolled over to starboard. The wheelhouse door slammed shut with a tremendous crash, and I was flung to the floor.

The engine had stopped but there was a pandemonium of noise outside the wheelhouse. Men were shouting and cursing and running along the deck. I heard the red fellow's voice raised above the rest, shouting: 'The dinghy! The dinghy!' Another voice, Long John's I think, bellowed: 'Back, curse you.' There was the sound of scuffling feet, the crunch of a heavy blow, and a scream of pain.

I struggled to my feet, hauling myself up on the compass mounting. The deck was at a crazy angle, so steep that it was all I could do to reach the door. I seized the handle and twisted it frantically. It would not open. I pushed and strained against it, striving to get a purchase on the sloping floor. The door would not budge. It had jammed tight.

I slid across to the opposite wall. The boat had canted at such an angle that I was almost standing on the wall. I peered out of the small window. The deck was awash, the sea surging against the wheelhouse.

Feet pounded past. There was more shouting and cursing. I scrambled back to the door, hammering on it desperately. It would not budge. There was a groaning of tortured timbers as the boat took on an even steeper list. I slid across the floor and crashed against the opposite wall. As I lay there I could hear the sea lapping against it.

There was no more shouting outside. The men must have taken to the dinghy. The boat shuddered and I felt the stern dip. She was fast on a reef, but it could be only a matter of minutes before she slid back into the sea. *Morgana* was doomed, and I was trapped with her.

Chapter Seventeen

Something crashed against the wheelhouse door. It shuddered from top to bottom. There was another blow. The door shook. I heard someone grunt, and a third blow rocked the door. The panel above the handle splintered and broke as the sharpened end of an iron bar forced a way through. The bar twisted and turned, directed by the hand outside for a leverage. It flattened back against the door and the panel bulged outwards. The wood splintered and cracked. There was a muffled exclamation outside. The door suddenly flew open.

Long John was at the opening. 'Look lively,' he shouted. 'She's near away.'

I scrambled up the steeply sloping floor and dashed out on deck. The stern of the boat and all her starboard side was under water, and the sea was lapping over the gunwale just outside the wheelhouse.

Long John had looped a length of cord to his crutch and was calmly knotting it. He slung the crutch over his shoulder. 'Can you swim?' he said.

I shook my head, looking around desperately. There was no sign of the dinghy. The nearest land I could see was at least thirty feet away, the point of a rocky headland. *Morgana* must have grounded on an underwater reef.

'Well, you will need to hang on to me,' Long John said. 'As long as you don't panic, we will manage fine.'

He hopped across the sloping deck and dropped straight over the side. He came up spitting water and shaking his dripping hair out of his eyes. 'Come on,' he shouted, catching the gunwale with one hand. 'Lively now before she goes.'

I lowered myself gingerly into the water, holding on tightly to the gunwale. My teeth started to chatter, as much from fright as the cold.

'Get a grip on my shoulders,' Long John said. 'You will be lying on your back, so keep your mouth shut. And lie still.'

I did not fancy letting go of the boat, but she gave a sudden lurch and settled deeper in the water. That decided it. I caught hold of Long John's broad shoulders, clutching at his woollen jersey.

'Not so tight, boy,' he protested. 'You are near choking me. Just take it easy. We have not far to go.'

He pushed off from the boat and struck out with a slow, powerful breast stroke. I was seized by a sudden panic at the start, as my face went under water. I wanted to clutch his neck and pull myself up, feeling that I must go under unless I got my head well clear of the water. But I fought my fear down, and lay still, keeping my head back.

'Fine,' he gasped, swimming strongly. 'Nearly there.'

Once I had found that I was not going to sink like a stone, it was not so bad. Indeed, it was all over just when I was settling down to it. He seized an overhanging spur of rock with his right hand, and supported my head with his left. I let go of his shoulders and grabbed the rock with both hands. 'Up you go,' he said, giving me a lift.

I pulled myself up out of the water and climbed on to the rock. It formed the tip of a jutting headland, the southern arm of a small cove.

'You can climb over the rocks,' Long John said. 'It is easier for me to swim to shore.'

He struck out again, swimming steadily for the shelving shore of the cove. I scrambled over the rocks, my sodden trousers clinging uncomfortably to my legs, and ran down to the water's edge to meet him. Before I could help him up, he had got his crutch off his back and was standing upright.

He shook himself like a dog coming out of the water and I doubt if the soaking troubled him any more than it would have troubled Lassie. He stumped off up the beach without a word to me.

There was a small strip of gritty sand, backed by a crescent of shingle, and then the ground rose steeply in a high, grassy bank. There were big boulders at the southern end of the bank, and a small stream wound down between them, and trickled slowly out to sea.

Long John stretched out on the grass, his back against a rock. I came up and stood beside him, squeezing out my sodden trousers. He pushed his dripping hair out of his eyes and looked back at *Morgana*. Only her bow and the top of her wheelhouse was showing now. As we watched she heeled over, and the wheelhouse dipped under water. Her bows came up and I caught a glimpse of her keel, as she slid off the hidden reef and vanished into the depths. A patch of oil was all that marked her grave, and the tide would soon shift that.

Long John pulled off his jersey and wrung it out. There was a long silence.

'I didn't mean to put her on the rocks,' I said, once I was certain he had no intention of speaking.

He took no heed and went on emptying his pockets. He laid his pipe and tobacco on the grass, and threw away a sodden box of matches.

'I was going to make for the gorge,' I said.

He had his big silver watch wrapped up in a handkerchief. He took it out and wiped the case dry, and held it up to his ear. It was going fine. I could hear the tick from where I was standing. He laid the watch down carefully on the grass.

'I was going to take her up the river,' I said, 'and beach

her below the bothy. That was my idea. I would have run for it.'

He took out a knife and started scraping at his pipe. I don't know why – he hadn't any dry matches.

'She would have been safe enough in the river,' I said. 'Just grounded. I didn't mean to wreck your boat. I only wanted to get away. They would have worried about me at home, see, not knowing where I was. And with Ruairidh bad, and everything, they have had enough to worry them without me missing.'

He blew down the stem of his pipe and shook it. 'Aye, that is right enough,' he said.

There was another awkward silence.

'It was the fellow called Harry who put me off course,' I said, when I could stand the silence no longer. 'I am not blaming him, mind. But he came round terrible quick after I had laid him out. He got me unawares. We were fighting when she went on the reef.'

'How did you lay him out?'

'With your salmon club,' I said hesitantly.

'Well, well,' he said, and laughed. Laughed! He was a queer man in some ways, Long John. If *Morgana* had been my boat, I could never have laughed.

'Did he get clear all right?' I said.

'Who? Harry?' He looked surprised, as if he had been listening with only half an ear. 'Aye, Harry got clear.'

'And the rest of them?'

His face darkened. 'Aye, the rest of them, too – led by the bold Munro. But I caught the same fellow a crack he will be nursing for many a day.' He chewed on his empty pipe for a while, then jabbed the stem out to the north-west. 'They are in the mist yonder, pulling like mad for the gorge. The red fellow will be hoping to seize the coble.'

'Will they come back for us?'

He laughed again, a bitter laugh this time. 'Not them,' he said. 'They are too busy trying to save their own miserable skins, boy.'

'Well, what are we going to do?' I said.

I thought afterwards that of all the strange things that

had happened to me, none was stranger than what took place right at the moment I asked that question.

'We stay right where we are,' Long John said quietly. 'In a few minutes you get taken home and I get carted to the jail.'

I thought he was joking, and I said so. He shook his head and pointed over my shoulder. A boat had loomed up out of the mist, a fishing boat by the look of her, and she was heading for the cove.

'The *Kingfisher*,' Long John said. 'Towing *Morgana*'s dinghy. Well, well, the bold boys didn't get far whatever.'

I wondered why he was so sure it was the jail for him, but I wondered no more when I saw the two uniformed policemen leaning over the bows. They came ashore in the dinghy. It was the same fellow at the oars who had been at the wheel when she had come to collect our catch.

'Kenny will be wild,' Long John said calmly, 'getting dragged out on the Sabbath by the police.' He chuckled. 'I am almost afraid to face him.'

He was certainly not afraid to face the police, no matter what he said about the skipper of the *Kingfisher*. He got to his feet as the two of them strode up the beach, and no fallen Emperor ever faced his captors with greater indifference.

I stood by his side, hardly knowing where to look. I wished I could hide myself, and not have to witness his shame. One of the policemen was a sergeant. He cleared his throat and said: 'Are you John MacGregor?'

'Aye, that's me,' Long John said.

The sergeant read out the charge and told him he was under arrest. I had always thought it was only done like that on the films, but no. They asked him if he had anything to say. He said no, all he wanted was a match.

He was taken below when we came aboard. I was going to follow him, but the sergeant said: 'Detective-Sergeant Cameron wants to see you. He is in the wheelhouse.'

I suppose I should have guessed by now, but I got the shock of my life when I saw the bald-headed stranger. There were scratches on his face, and his head was bandaged, but he looked none the worse for his accident.

'Come in,' he said, as I stood gaping at the door. 'I shan't eat you. Perhaps I should have told you who I was that night at the river, but I wasn't too sure of you. No wonder I thought I had seen you before. You are Ruairidh's brother, aren't you?'

I nodded.

'I could see the resemblance,' he said. 'Well, you'll be pleased to know he is a lot better. They tell me he is sitting up and demanding to know how long he has to stay in bed.'

I was pleased right enough, but his news did not stir me the way I had imagined it would. I had too much on my mind to be really happy about anything. Ruairidh would be the first one to appreciate that.

The detective told me he had first met Ruairidh years ago, when he had been after an army deserter who was on the same ship as him. And he told me how he had come to be hunting the salmon poachers.

The police had become suspicious of the regular weekly visits of *Morgana* to lonely Loch Duich. They had discovered that Long John was her owner, and that he was working at the salmon fishing. When Sergeant Cameron had found that Ruairidh was a member of the crew, he had asked him to keep an eye on Long John.

'Once I heard that Ruairidh had met with an accident, I knew that MacGregor was up to no good,' he said.

'But that was the work of Murdo, the Harris man,' I said quickly.

'Another rogue, and a bad one,' he said. 'Oddly enough, Ruairidh was on the same boat as him a year or two back. He was suspected of stealing from his shipmates, but the police were never able to prove it.'

'Well, you have got him now,' I said, 'and a good thing too. That is one fellow I am not sorry to see making straight for the jail.'

'Hospital first,' he said. 'I think he has a broken shoulder. I gather that old rogue MacGregor was laying about him with his crutch.'

I told him how Long John had tried to stop them making off in the dinghy, when I was trapped in the wheelhouse of the sinking *Morgana*, and how he had stayed behind and saved my life.

He was a good listener and he encouraged me to go on, not that I fancied talking freely to a policeman, but it was different with him, seeing he was not wearing the uniform. I told him everything that had happened from the time I had gone in the ambulance with Ruairidh to the hospital, and I put in a good word for Long John, although I was standing behind Kenny, the skipper of the *Kingfisher*, and the same fellow's ears were flapping plenty. Well, he could tell the Laird for all I cared. I was speaking the truth.

I was still talking when the *Kingfisher* nosed slowly into the river mouth. The policeman in the bow heaved the anchor over the side, and the boat swung round slowly on the tide.

'Good life!' I exclaimed, looking out at the familiar bothy, and the beached coble. 'I thought we were making for Portree.'

'Too risky,' the detective said.

Kenny, the skipper, spoke for the first time. 'Aye, the mist is coming in fast,' he said. 'It is out of the question to chance it at sea.'

The detective jerked his head in the direction of the gorge. 'I have a van waiting for them at the top,' he said.

I stepped outside the wheelhouse. The mist was not so thick as it had been in the morning, but I could not see much beyond the bridge, and it was wreathed around the tops of the poles on the drying green. Across the Sound, thick white banks of it were rolling in again from the east.

The uniformed sergeant came up from below. I knew there was something wrong the moment I clapped eyes on him. He brushed past me, and leaned inside the wheelhouse. 'We will need to get a doctor,' I heard him say to the detective. 'It's MacGregor. He is in a bad way.'

Chapter Eighteen

I was down on my knees beside the bunk they had laid him on, watching him anxiously. The frothing around his mouth had stopped, but his face looked grey. His eyes were closed. Only the slight rise and fall of his chest showed that he was still living.

The rest of them had been ferried ashore in the dinghy. The red fellow had protested that he was not fit to climb out of the gorge, and indeed, he looked in a bad shape. His right arm hung limply at his side, and he could hardly draw one foot after the other.

But the detective had beckoned to Kenny, the skipper. Kenny had hooked the red fellow's good arm over his broad shoulder, and he took him along, not too gently at that. The other two were guarded by the uniformed policemen, and the detective had gone for a doctor. He had told me that he thought Long John had taken a heart attack.

I had rowed straight back to the *Kingfisher*, once the party had started the climb out of the gorge, hoping he would be better, but he had lain like a dead man ever since I had tiptoed up to his bunk.

His eyes flickered open. He gazed around, like a man in a daze. 'Have they all gone, boy?' he said.

'Aye, but the bald one will soon be back with a doctor,' I said.

He groaned. Flecks of foam appeared on his lips. I picked up the towel from the bunk and wiped his mouth.

'Is the pain bad?' I asked.

'Bad enough,' he said. He moistened his lips. 'Niall.'

'Aye.'

'Maybe one day, you and me, we'll try the shark fishing, eh?'

'Aye, surely,' I said bravely, hoping he would not die on me before the doctor came.

He frowned, as if he had suddenly remembered something that pained him. 'We will need a new boat, though,' he said weakly, and his lips twisted, so that you would have almost thought he was smiling, had he not been in pain.

I nodded dumbly.

He put out a hand and gripped my arm. '*Morgana* was done, anyway,' he said. 'We will have a better boat next time, you and me.'

'Aye.'

He licked his lips. 'Niall, will you make over to the bothy for me? There is a bottle o' rum in the kitchen. A sip o' rum would put me right. Better than all the doctors.'

'I saw the red fellow put it in his pocket when we left this morning,' I said, hating to have to disappoint him.

His eyes closed, and the froth started again on his lips. I wiped his mouth dry. 'Another bottle,' he murmured. 'Hidden in my bunk. In the blankets.' He opened his eyes again. 'Will you get it for me, Niall?'

'Surely,' I said. I pushed the towel into his hands. 'Just you lie still. I won't be a minute.'

I rushed up on deck and dropped into the dinghy. Casting off, I seized the oars and rowed like mad upstream to the bothy. I ran inside and clambered up on his bunk, patting the blankets. There was no bottle there. I stripped off all the blankets, but I still could not find it. I tried the other three bunks, just in case he had been mistaken, but there was not a bottle of rum hidden in any of them. He was probably delirious, and rambling.

I stood in the centre of the floor, wondering how I would break the news to him. At that moment the engine of the *Kingfisher* started up.

I raced outside. Long John was moving about inside the wheelhouse. I ran down the river bank until I was level with the boat. A stump of rope was hanging over the bow, where it had been cut free from the anchor.

He saw me. He pushed back the sliding window and stuck his head out of the wheelhouse. He was grinning from ear to ear.

'What are you doing?' I yelled. 'You should be lying down.'

'A MacGregor never lies down,' he said, 'not until there is six feet o' cold earth on his chest, or fifty fathoms o' water, more like. I am off, Niall, so good luck to you, boy.'

'But you are ill,' I protested.

'Not me,' he laughed. 'I chewed on a bit of soap just. An old dodge that, boy.'

'But the mist,' I said. 'You will never make it.'

'Better the mist than the jail for me,' he said. 'I will take my chance, like I have always done.'

He withdrew his head. I thought he was off, but he thrust his arm out of the window and cried: 'Catch!' It was a knotted handkerchief and I caught it easily, for I was less than ten feet from him.

He bent over the wheel and the note of the engine deepened. The screw churned the water. 'I am leaving you the only enemy,' he shouted, and he thrust out his arm, and waved.

The *Kingfisher* headed straight out to sea. In less than a minute she was lost in the mist. I stood there stupidly, clutching the handkerchief in my fist, gazing after her. The note of her engine had faded in the distance before I realized that I had not even waved to him.

I looked down at the big brown handkerchief in my hand, and I started to unpick the knots. My nails were too short, and I had to take my teeth to them. I got them undone, and unwrapped the handkerchief. Inside it was Long John's silver pocket watch. I held it up to my ear. It had a strong tick.

Standing there at the river mouth, with the watch in my hand, I looked out across the Sound. The mist had almost reached the water at my feet, great swirling clouds of thick white vapour. There was not a rock or a reef in the Sound that would not be hidden by it. And there were score upon score of rocks and reefs lying in wait for the *Kingfisher*.

It was the Sabbath Day, and I thought of His disciples, Simon and James and John, who had left their nets to become fishers of men. The Lord would surely look kindly upon a fisherman. I shut my eyes, and said a prayer.